"Okay," he said with resolve, "we're going to have to be good actors in the days ahead. No one, I mean, *no one*, can know how we feel about each other. Go home and pretend you're not even thinking about me. We won't talk until the Halloween dance."

On the way home in the bus I looked out the window at all the familiar streets of Bar Ferry, the police station, the library, even the hospital where I was born, and thought: Not until I met Harvey did I realize that for fifteen years I'd been bored and lonely. I didn't feel that way anymore.

Do You Love Me, Harvey Burns?

Jean Marzollo

SCHOLASTIC INC.

New York Toronto London Auckland Sydney Tokyo

For CM
With special thanks to Amy Erlich, my editor

And thanks also to
Robert, Jack, and David Byrnes,
Carol Carson, Kate McMullan,
Mary Pope Osborne, and Sunny Rhodes
for many helpful suggestions

ISBN 0-590-33192-2

12 11 10 9 8 7 6 5 4 3 2 1   9   4 5 6 7 8 9/8

Part I

"Hello?"

"It's me."

"Hi, Denise."

"Whatcha doing?"

"Reading *Wuthering Heights*."

"On the afternoon of our first senior high school dance?" Denise has no sense of humor. Of course I wasn't reading *Wuthering Heights*. There was a long pause. "I called Clearlight," she said. Another pause. Denise always pauses. "She's got new reptile print pumps."

"Pumps?"

"Flats."

"Mm-m."

"What?"

"Nothing." Denise was waiting for me to ask what else Clearlight was wearing, but I wouldn't ask. Let's face it, girls, like chickens, have a pecking order. Denise has better clothes than I do, but I'm smarter. As long as we pretend I don't care about clothes and she doesn't care about brains, we are even.

"You're coming over here first, right?" she asked.

"Right."

"Are you nervous?"

"Not particularly."

She sighed. "I hope we get boyfriends this year. I'm sick of being a late bloomer, aren't you?"

I wasn't pleased to be categorized with her as a late bloomer, but it seemed pointless to protest. "Che sarà, sarà," I said, staring at the bouquets of wheat printed on my mother's bedspread. The only upstairs phone in our house is on her night table. Denise has her own phone, a red Princess, in her room.

"What does that mean?"

"Che sarà, sarà. You know: whatever will be, will be."

"It sounds so risky," Denise said. She sighed again. "What are you wearing?"

"I haven't thought of it yet."

"Well, Clearlight's wearing lavender baggy jeans, a white Victorian blouse, and, like I said, reptile print flats. I'm wearing a new blue sweater with puffy sleeves, new pink baggies, and new pink ballerina flats. You haven't thought about your outfit at all? You'd better get going. Why don't you copy Clearlight too? You've got baggies and flats."

Clearlight. Clearlight Jones. One of the most beautiful girls in Bar Ferry. She's a junior. Because she lives in the Rivergate development with me and Denise, the three of us sort of hang around. At least Denise and I like to think of it that way. All the girls envy Clearlight. When she looks at herself in the mirror, Clearlight must feel something like the warmth of the sun. Maybe that's why her parents named her Clearlight, though how could they have known she would grow up to be so beautiful? She says they called her Clearlight because they were hippies when she was born. She doesn't care. She likes to be different.

"Lisa, why don't you say anything?"

"What? Oh, I'm sorry. I was just thinking of Heathcliff."

"Heath who?"

"Heathcliff. He's in *Wuthering Heights*. He's got a craggy face. I might do a drawing of him."

"How can you think about art on a day like today?"

"Easy," I said. Then I realized I'd been a little snotty, so I changed my tone. "Denise?"

"Yeah?"

I didn't know what I wanted to say. Something friendly. "I can't wait to see your outfit."

· 2 ·

I returned to my room and took out my red plaid Victorian blouse, denim baggies, and red flats. I placed them in a row on my bed and thought: Why, they're nothing but pieces of a uniform. All I get to pick is the color. I looked at myself in the mirror with disgust. I'd better get going. I'd better wash my hair and curl it with a curling iron so it will look just like Denise's and Donna's and Beth's. We all do our hair exactly the same way. But not Clearlight. Her hair is naturally long, thick, black, curly, soft, and shiny.

I opened my third drawer and pulled out from under my sweater pile an article I had torn out of one of Denise's fashion magazines. It said that personal style was a way of communicating to the world who you were, and it said girls should dare to be bold. Another page showed step by step how to frizz your hair.

"Whatever you experience is the truth, so I experience myself as beautiful," Clearlight had announced at the last pajama party. That was excellent advice, I thought, and I vowed to start following it. Tonight I was going to experience myself as different and beautiful. The first step was to wash my hair and plait it into fifty tight braids.

· 3 ·

Downstairs the back door slammed. My father had come in singing "Tomorrow," the theme song from *Annie*. I had to laugh. I was ten when he had taken us to see that show. That was five years ago, for heaven's sake, yet he was still singing the hit tune. Corny as the lyrics were, I sang along softly and watched myself in the mirror. I had dried my braids so thoroughly that when I undid them, my hair was completely crimped. Then I brushed it until it shone and fluffed out sideways. Now I put two barrettes on each side, four in all, just like the models in the magazine.

There. I looked in the mirror and pretended I had just entered a Hollywood restaurant filled with famous people. They stood up and cheered. "What? A party for me?" I threw up my hands in startled joy. Maybe I really *did* look fabulous, especially when I tilted my head just so.

It was going to be a fine evening. Something would happen. I wasn't sure what it would be, but Clearlight promised senior high dances were different from junior high dances, where boys stood on one side of the gym and girls stood on the other. I couldn't wait for her and Denise to see me. For a final touch I took a red cloth rose that came on another blouse and pinned it to my plaid shirt. Now I looked perfect.

My father was on the phone with his back to me. He was wearing a gray sweat shirt with the arms cut off, faded overalls, and work boots. He's a contractor; at least that's what I write down on forms. Basically what he does is build houses one at a time for New Yorkers who are moving beyond the suburbs to our part of the Hudson River valley. Some of them he knows from advertising, which he quit a few years ago because he couldn't stand the two-hour commute to the city.

"Hello," he was saying. "This is Bill Barnes from Bar Ferry. Say, I saw your ad for a 'sixty-eight Volkswagen' in *The Pennysaver*, and I was wondering if I might run over tomorrow morning to take a look at it."

He also reconditions old cars and sells them. It's his opinion that preemission-control VWs were the best cars ever made. He's always talking about them to anyone who will listen.

I crossed quietly behind my father to the refrigerator and took out a glass baking dish containing six raw drumsticks covered with crushed cornflakes. I've been doing most of the cooking ever since my mother started working. In the morning, she tells me what to do and I have no choice but to do exactly as she says. If I don't she has a fit.

This morning, when she told me to rub chicken legs with Crisco and dip them in crushed cornflakes, I looked at her and wondered if she had forgotten all about the dance. That would be like her these days. I can tell you I hated to get that Crisco on my fingers, and the way it felt to spread it on cold chicken was gross. I did it as soon as I got home.

"Okeydoke, I'll be over to Fairley tomorrow morning at ten. . . . Right, right. . . . Don't worry, I'll find it. . . . Fine, fine. . . . Bye now." My father hung up the phone.

I put the chicken in the oven, set the dial to 400 degrees, and crossed the floor to the table. I was aware that my father was staring at me.

"Well, well," he said, looking at my hair, then looking away.

"There's a dance tonight. It's the first dance of the year." I glanced over and saw him raise his eyebrows, suck in his breath, hold it, and then let it out slowly as if he were blowing up a balloon. "My first senior high school dance," I added, hoping he would know enough to say something right.

"Well, well, well," he said again, folding his arms across his chest and leaning back against the counter. "I remember my first high school dance." My father smiled at the wall above my head as if it were an old friend. "It was in 1959. Freddy Thompson and I smuggled in a live chicken and let it go in the middle of the dance floor, right next to Betty Alberts."

My father shut his eyes and chuckled, first shaking his head back and forth as if the wall were saying, "Go on, you didn't," and then nodding up and down as if to reply, "Oh, yes, we did. I'm afraid we did."

"Dad," I said, trying to laugh and wondering if he liked the way I looked.

My mother came in, carrying a bag of groceries and her blue vinyl briefcase. Her eyes darted back and forth from my father to the stove to me, and I knew she was finding so many things wrong she didn't know where to start. She heaved her things up onto the counter.

"Did you stop at the cleaner's?" she asked my father.

"What? Oh, gosh, Heather, I forgot. I'm sorry, I'll stop tomorrow. I saw an ad in *The Pennysaver*, and I wanted to get right home and —"

"Lisa, did you put the chicken in? Okay, I smell it. Did you start the rice? It's five forty-five."

"I was just going to," I said.

"Bill, did you call my mother?"

"Yes," said my father. "I did that. She said to thank you for the candy you sent."

"How was she feeling?"

"She said she was feeling okay, but that she missed seeing us on her birthday."

My mother frowned at the groceries and began to unpack. I started to measure a cup of dry rice. When I bent down to get the rice pan, I could feel my hair lift as a whole unit and fall back down on my head. I measured the water and put the pan on the stove.

"You going somewhere special?" my mother asked.

"Just a dance," I mumbled, wondering what was going to happen next. I saw my father get a beer and sneak out of the room.

"How are you getting there?" she asked.

"Denise," I said.

"I wasn't aware that Denise had a license," she said, cramming vegetables into the crisper bin.

"Denise's mother," I said, pouring rice into the boiling water. I picked up a spoon and stirred the rice so it wouldn't stick. Then I replaced the cover and lowered the heat.

I have read that frogs have transparent eyelids that they pull over their eyes when they swim underwater. When my mother gets a certain tense way, I pull something like a transparent lid over my whole brain. Then what happens is that I see what's going on around me, but I don't feel it.

"Are you trying to tell me Denise's mother is taking you to the dance and picking you up as well?"

"Yes."

"Well, all right," said my mother, taking off her trench coat. "But make sure you are home early."

"Mrs. Hall said she would take us to Victor's Palace after." Victor's Palace is a fast-food place with a parking lot and good french fries. Kids hang out there.

"I swear I don't know where some women get all the energy." My mother sunk her coat on a hook and sighed. She rubbed her face as if she were washing it; then she spread her fingers across her cheekbones and looked at my shoes, pants, blouse, flower, and hair.

I raised my hands nervously and set them down lightly on the top of my head. I could feel exactly where my hair was straight and where the frizzed part started.

"I guess the reason," my mother said, "that Mrs. Hall can bake cakes for every town bazaar, keep her garden blooming in late September, and chauffeur teenage girls to dances and snack bars is that she doesn't have a job. Not that I mind getting out of the house. I'm just making a point."

Having made it, my mother dropped her hands into her skirt pockets and headed for the bathroom. I didn't know if *she* liked the way I looked either.

· 4 ·

Our dining room table is made of thick taffy-colored wood with rounded edges. The place mats are worn plastic-laminated photographs of places in New England where we used to go on trips. Mine shows the aerial tramway in New Hampshire with a cutaway shot of the Old Man of the Mountains. My mother has a map of Cape Cod on hers, and my father has the Bennington Battle Monument on his. I don't know why we never switch our mats around.

We never switch seats either. I always sit facing the kitchen, and my mother and father always sit on the ends facing each other. That night, as usual, there was tension in the air. Slowly and tediously my mother was lifting small forkfuls of coleslaw to her mouth, as if each mouthful were a burden she had no choice but to bear. She had changed out of her office clothes and was in her green velour bathrobe. Her hair was down, and there was a long, unnatural kink in it from the elastic band she had worn under her bun all day.

My father was smacking rice against the

roof of his mouth. "I believe I found another Beetle," he said, "Beetle" being his way of conveying to us that he was in a pretty good mood, one that he hoped would be contagious.

I was going around my plate cautiously, one bite at a time. Chicken, rice, coleslaw, chicken, rice, coleslaw.

My mother looked up but didn't say a word. She was worried about money, I knew. She worked for an insurance agency and had liked her job until last year, when she got a new boss. I considered asking her how things were going but couldn't think of a safe way to do it.

"Quality in cars is the name of the game," said my father. He smiled at us, then looked at the ceiling and sighed. He seemed to give up. We all just sat there and chewed.

With my left hand I reached up and touched the small cool round drawer pull in front of me. It was hard to believe we once had fun in this room. Generally I tried not to think about the past, but at moments like this, when all I could hear was chewing, I sometimes thought I would scream. I sometimes imagined I would grip the table so hard my fingers would turn white, and I would ask in a searing voice, "Why don't we go to shows like *Annie* anymore? Why did you sell the piano that was in the corner of the room? Why don't we sing and dance around the table anymore? Why don't you ever get excited anymore? Why don't you at least tell me if I look all right and wish me luck?"

But this was only in my mind. I'm not the screaming type. I'm the type who thinks things and remembers.

"Bill." My mother set her fork down on her plate, which was made, like all of ours, of thick dark green plastic. The impact of fork against plate made a loud, hollow sound. "Can't you relax?"

My father looked up. "What?"

"I can't stand how fast you eat."

"Am I eating too fast? I beg your pardon." He looked at me and shrugged.

"I'd just like to have a peaceful dinner for once," said my mother.

"Hey, no problem," he said, leaning back against his chair and patting his stomach. He seemed ready to have another try at family harmony. "You know, Lisa," he began, "your mother and I used to go to The Four Jays after our high school dances. You know that run-down place on Route Fifty-two? Well, it sure was hopping then."

He winked at me, and I squeezed the drawer pull out of nervousness. It wasn't going to work, this move of his. He was only going to make a fool of himself, and that would make my mother madder.

"Things haven't changed so much," said my father wistfully, emptying a beer can into his glass, "though I can tell you, it sure feels strange to have my daughter going off to her first high school dance. I guess your mom and I could still cut a few figures on the dance floor. What about it, Heather? And remember how you used to iron your hair to make it straight?"

My mother covered up a small smile with her napkin. But then she smiled again as if she couldn't help it. I pulled the drawer toward me about an inch and felt confused. What was she smiling at?

"I guess I'll be going," I said, getting up.

"But you have to do the dishes," said my mother.

"And you have to fix your hair," said my father. "I mean, don't you? That's not the way you're really going to wear it, is it?"

My mother put her head back and laughed out loud. Surprised but pleased that his words had amused her, my father joined in. Then they stopped, but it was too late. I was mortified.

"It *is* the way she's going to wear it, Bill," said my mother, trying to be serious. "That's the latest fashion."

"I'm sorry, Lisa," said my father, a little bewildered. "I didn't know. I guess it looks nice, but, well, it's just that I like your hair plain, that's all." He looked at my mother. "And I think your mother does too."

"Plain?" I asked, rising slowly and gripping the table until my fingers turned white. *"Plain?"*

In my mind I pushed the table over, but all I actually did was walk out of the room on shaky legs and run upstairs to my room.

Plain? I'll give them plain, I said to myself.

My father was outside the door. "Lisa, I'm sorry. It's just that . . . Lee, baby, we didn't mean to laugh at you. Come on down. Let me take another look."

What a phony he was, but I didn't bother to tell him that. I didn't bother to ask him why the only time the two of them ever laughed together was when they laughed at me or if that was their way of saying, "Have a great time." When I heard him go back downstairs, I opened my door quietly and stood at the top of the stairs.

"Bill," I heard my mother say, "she's in a typical teenage phase. We mustn't give in to it. She's got to learn that temper tantrums won't get her anywhere."

· 5 ·

I ran into the bathroom and looked in the mirror. My hair looked so stupid I wanted to die. I hated it. I hated them too. Plain? How would they like me with my hair cut off? In a fury I opened the medicine cabinet, seized the scissors, and chopped some hair in the back right off. Chunk, chunk, I cut off two more huge, long pieces. If it's plain they want, they'll *love* ugly. All of a sudden I grabbed the scissors with both hands and felt I had enough strength to stab the point right through the sink. Then the sensation passed.

I set the scissors on the edge of the sink and felt weak. Well, I thought, strangely satisfied, at least I don't have to try anymore.

Now my hair will look so bad that *no* one will ask me to dance. And I don't really care. There's more to life than dances. I can read, I can draw, and I have thoughts no one knows about.

"Never throw hair into the toilet," my father always says. I scooped up all the hair from the sink and flushed it down, hoping the toilet would back up while I was gone.

Matter-of-factly I took another shower and partially dried my hair. Actually it didn't look as bad as I thought it would. By some miracle the cut off sections were underneath in the back. I guess I knew all along they were there, but at the time I had felt completely out of control. I took out my curling iron and curled the sides of my hair and my bangs the way everyone else did. I have to admit I was somewhat relieved to know that now I wouldn't stand out.

It was time to meet Denise. I ran downstairs, yelled good-bye, grabbed my jacket, and closed the door behind me before I could hear whether anyone replied or not.

Outside, it was cool and dark. I ran for a block, then walked and looked up at the sky. Stars always calm me down. The closest star is about four and a half light-years away. There are more than a billion galaxies, and each one of them has more than a billion stars. At one number per second, it would take thirty-two years to count to a billion. If I started counting the night of my first senior high dance, I wouldn't finish until I was forty-seven. By that time I wouldn't even remember frizzing my hair.

• 6 •

Denise's mother was taking pictures of Denise in front of the fireplace. Denise's new blue sweater complemented her red hair wonderfully, but I wasn't jealous because Denise was a little plump. No matter how much her mother helped her and how little my mother helped me, the fact remained that Denise and I were at the same place on the personal appearance scale (above average, below beautiful). This was probably the main reason we were friends.

"Come on in, Lisa, and have your picture taken with Denise," said Mrs. Hall.

"No, that's all right."

"Oh, come on now. Take off your jacket and let me see you."

I took off my jacket and dropped it on the gold velvet couch.

"Isn't that a *nice* rose?" said Mrs. Hall. "And your hair looks *so* clean."

I stepped over, and Denise put her arm around my waist.

"Okay, now, say 'Cheez Whiz,'" said Mrs. Hall. "Oh, come on, Lisa. You can do better than that."

I tried to smile but couldn't very well.

"That's enough flashcubes for one evening," said Mrs. Hall. "Do you know how much they *cost*?"

Denise and I went up to her room. She had a Snoopy bedspread, a Snoopy clock, and a huge cross-stitched wall hanging of Snoopy in his doghouse. Woodstock was on top, the balloon reading HOME SWEET HOME. Mrs. Hall had made it for Denise's fifteenth birthday. I couldn't believe Denise actually hung it up.

Denise was standing sideways in front of her full-length mirror. "Do you think this sweater makes me look fat?" she asked.

I sat down on the bed and tried to be diplomatic. "Well, the puffy sleeves probably make you *feel* fat, but they don't actually make you *look* fat. That shade of blue is great for redheads."

"I don't know," said Denise, pouting.

"Well, change if you don't like it," I said.

She plucked at the front of her sweater several times, then rearranged the band around her waist. "I just don't know," she said again. "What about these pants? Do you think *they* make me look fat?"

There was a little tap on the door. "Girls, may I come in?" Before we could answer, Mrs. Hall entered. She went over and rearranged Denise's sweater yet again, fluffing the puffy sleeves Denise had just tried to flatten. "Isn't this a dreamy sweater?" she asked.

"Sure is," I said.

"And you, Lisa, why, I think I have just the thing for you. Stand up."

Mrs. Hall ran out of the room and returned with a new red cinch belt. "Try this, Lisa. It'll be the final touch on your outfit. I bought it for me and Denise, but it's not exactly our thing, I'm afraid. But you, you're so thin. There. It's perfect."

Mrs. Hall had put it on me, and now she stood back so I could look at myself in Denise's long mirror. She was right. The cinch belt *was* perfect. Suddenly I had confidence again in me and the evening.

"You both look so nice I'm sure you're going to have a wonderful time." Mrs. Hall squeezed her hands in front of her chest and beamed. "Your first senior high dance. It's a milestone, isn't it? And to think," she said, hugging Denise, "that I remember the day you were born as if it was yesterday. It was 5:05 A.M. I had been in labor for . . . oh, well, I'm sure you don't want to hear that now." Mrs. Hall put her hand to her eyes and brushed away a tear.

I wasn't jealous of Denise, but I was jealous of her mother. Mrs. Hall told Denise everything she wanted to know. My mother, if she just came out and told me she didn't like me, that would be bad enough, but at least then I would know. The way it was in our house, sometimes I got the feeling she just didn't care one way or the other about me. I shook my head and looked down, putting my hands on my waist and feeling the strong stretch of spandex.

"What's the matter, Lisa?" asked Mrs. Hall.

"Nothing," I said with a sigh. "This belt feels great. Thanks."

"Tell you what," said Mrs. Hall. "Let's all have a piece of pie before leaving."

"No, thank you," I mumbled. My throat was sore from trying not to cry.

"Are you sure? Positive?"

"Let's just go and get it over with!" said Denise a little desperately.

"How are your folks, Lisa?" asked Mrs. Hall in the car.

"Fine," I said.

"Your mom enjoying her job?"

"I guess so."

"I don't know where she gets all that marvelous energy," said Mrs. Hall.

· 7 ·

The high school gym reminded me of a big dark cave. Kids flitted in and out of the exit doors like moths.

Denise and I found Clearlight talking with a bunch of girls like Donna Serwinski and Beth Hanson, whom I knew from last year, and others like Nancy Bettelson and Lorrie White from the other junior high. Clearlight was telling everyone that she washes her hair with detergent. No one could believe it.

"You mean like Joy?" asked Nancy.

"If there's no shampoo," said Clearlight mysteriously.

"Oh, so what you mean is that if you run out of shampoo, you use detergent," said

Lorrie, trying to get to the bottom of the matter.

"I'm saying it doesn't really make any difference," said Clearlight.

I reached up to make sure the chopped-off ends of my hair were still under those that had been spared. If Clearlight had attacked her hair the way I had, she probably would be telling everyone about it now, but of course, if it were *her* hair, it would have come out great and become the latest style.

Rick Widmer, one of the most popular juniors, came over and asked Clearlight to dance. We stared at the backs of their two heads, hers so black and his so blond.

"It's freezing in here," I said.

"Really," said Denise. "And they don't have a band."

"It's just like junior high," said Donna in disgust.

The music stopped. Kids walked by. My group, now that Clearlight was gone, was not doing well. I tried to look positive and perky, but inside I felt leaden. I didn't know if I could stand senior high if the dances were as bad as they were in junior high. Waiting on the sidelines made it hard to experience myself as different and beautiful.

"Let's go to the girls' room," said Donna.

I said I'd stay because I just couldn't stand to move across the floor with a herd of unpicked girls. Denise stayed with me. It seemed we stood there, just the two of us, for hours. I don't know why I started telling

Denise that I had killed a frog in advanced biology. I should have known she wouldn't have been interested. But somehow, standing there on the edge of the gym, my frog was all I could think of.

"The amazing thing was I didn't mind killing it," I said. "I mean I knew I was killing something alive, but I figured how bad can death be if it's instant? Some of the kids didn't stick the rod into the back of the frog's head fast enough. *Their* frogs were the ones that suffered."

"Really," said Denise abstractedly, looking over my shoulder.

I could have pinched her. The music stopped, and I stopped talking. I may have looked as if I were still talking, though, because I had my mouth half-open in a frozen, frantic smile, hoping I would get asked to dance before I went out of my mind.

The music started up, and the girls were coming back. I was looking at some tenth-grade boys joking by the bleachers when Denise told me that the apple pie her mother had baked had no apples in it. Just Ritz crackers. My mind did a double take. Had Denise just said her mother had made an apple pie with no apples in it? What was she talking about?

"I couldn't tell one bit," she continued. "That's why she asked you if you wanted a piece — to see if you could tell."

Bobby O'Brien was heading toward us. He lived two blocks from me. In third grade I had beat him up, but now I smiled at him. Boy, did I smile! Then an awful thing happened. Bobby asked Denise to dance.

I felt the whole room was watching me, so I began to walk across the floor as if I had seen an old friend. My heart was pounding with embarrassment, yet I kept on smiling.

And then, and this is true, I swear it, the crowd of kids in front of me seemed to part, and I saw a tall boy heading straight for me. He had short thick brown hair and was grinning at me in a half-friendly, half-mocking way as if he knew my smile was fake. He stopped right in front of me, closer than you would think a stranger would come.

"Oh," I said. "Excuse me."

"Why should I excuse you?" he asked. "You didn't do anything. Follow me."

I followed him to the very center of the dance floor, where he turned and held out his arms, and I saw all these things at once: his black watch plaid shirt — how ironed it was — his navy blue Shetland sweater, the thick kind of good wool sweater that sells at the Tweede Shoppe for sixty dollars, a Casio computer watch on his wrist, and Clearlight waving as she danced by.

The boy put one hand on the small of my back and held his other hand up higher than most boys do. His palm was dry and slightly calloused. He held me not too close and led me around the dance floor without talking.

Clearlight danced by again with her eyebrows raised in a look of surprised approval.

One of my favorite old songs was playing, "In My Room" by the Beach Boys. I hummed along, harmonizing without thinking. Then I stopped, embarrassed, hoping the boy hadn't heard me. I wondered if he was an upperclassman and if Clearlight knew his name.

· 8 ·

When the music ended, the boy kept his arm around my waist.

"You're a good dancer," he said.

"Thanks," I said. He had braces.

"My name's Harvey Burns," he said.

"Mine's Lisa. Lisa Barnes."

"Burns. Barnes," he said.

"Sounds like someone should call the fire department," I said. I couldn't believe I had made a joke, just like that.

He had a sharp, open laugh and didn't seem at all embarrassed about his braces or anything.

"Hey, Harve, robbing the cradle?" asked someone with a thick, husky voice. A big blond boy lurched past. I felt my face get hot, but Harvey just laughed.

"Moose Dubinsky," said Harvey. "His locker is next to mine. You know him?"

"Not really," I said. I wanted to make another joke, something about a moose, but I couldn't think of one. I chuckled anyway.

"You don't like him, I can tell," said Harvey. "Neither do I."

I shrugged my shoulders because I felt stupid talking about someone I didn't know.

Then, without saying anything, we were dancing again. I did know how to dance pretty well because when I was little, I danced with my father. That was when we had a piano and my mother used to play.

But in junior high I had learned that kids weren't supposed to dance fancy, so I had trained myself to dance like the other kids, step, step, step, in no particular direction or design. Just be glad you got picked, and for God's sake, don't lead.

But this guy Harvey, he could really dance. He rested his chin lightly on the top of my head, and around the dance floor we went, circling past the other couples. Kids started watching. I wasn't sure if they liked it or not. Once I saw Denise's face in the crowd, and she looked impressed, but then again she would be.

There was more and more room on the dance floor because dancers were moving back. I could hardly believe what was happening. I was afraid if I let myself get embarrassed, I might miss a step, but I didn't, mostly because Harvey seemed so relaxed. He sure had a lot of self-confidence. I could tell he was really enjoying himself. More than that, I could feel he was holding himself up in a certain aristocratic way as if to say, "You and I are in a world of our own."

As for me, I was thrilled. Whirling around the dance floor with Harvey was the happiest moment of my life, and I never wanted it to end. But it did end, and when it was over, I heard kids clapping. Denise ran over.

"Lisa!" she exclaimed, looking up at Harvey.

"Denise," I was getting ready to say, "this is Harvey Burns. Harvey, this is Denise Hall." I was even going to do the Burns Barnes joke for her, but I never got a chance because Harvey just said, "Thank you," and with that same strange grin he'd had when I first saw him, he turned and walked away.

· 9 ·

My first thought was to kill Denise. Then to kill myself. Then to kill Harvey.

"Who *is* he?" asked Denise.

I took a deep breath. "Harvey Burns. I don't know." I smoothed down the back of my hair over the short pieces. "He has braces."

"So? He sure is a good dancer."

"He's okay," I said. I could hardly breathe. I was dying to turn around and see where Harvey went. Bobby O'Brien and Tommy DeNoto came over. Bobby asked Denise to dance again and Tommy asked me.

I've known Tommy all my life. He's my age. In junior high he got the award for best athlete. He had never paid much attention to girls, so I guess I was surprised when he asked me to dance. Half an hour earlier I would have been thrilled, but now I could hardly pay attention to him. Out of the corner of my eyes I saw Harvey dancing with Ellen Goldberg. She had her hair in one long, thick braid and was laughing. Harvey was laughing too.

"I see your dad's adding on to his store," I said to Tommy. "What's he putting in the new part?"

"More tools," said Tommy.

"Really?" I tried to look fascinated. "What kind of tools? Is he getting in a new line or something?"

"I don't know," said Tommy, stepping on my right toe. "Oops, sorry."

"That's okay," I said. "Well, the addition looks pretty good, I think." I wish it were a fast dance so at least Tommy and I could move separately.

"You want to dance again?" he asked when the record was over. "I mean, I know I'm not as good as Burns."

"Burns? You know him?"

"He went out for football and was going to kick field goals, but something happened. He got in a fight with someone and quit."

"A fight? Quit?" That didn't sound like the boy I had just danced with. "What year is he?" I asked nonchalantly, putting my arms up to dance.

"Junior."

This time Tommy and I danced close. Step, step, step, boring, boring, boring. Slowly we inched our way across the floor with our ears pressed together. Life was so weird. Earlier in the afternoon I would have died for this. Now all I could think of was Harvey Burns, who used to be on the football team and who had been in a fight. I wondered what would make him fight, and I hated to think about his getting hurt. Step, step, step. I also wondered why I had to put up with walking to music when I loved so much to dance.

Tommy and I eventually reached the other side of the floor, and as we made a slow turn, I happened to glance up. There was Harvey, sitting at the top of the bleachers all by himself. His legs were stretched out on the bench in front of him, his elbows were resting on the bench behind him, and his eyes were right on me. We kept turning, Tommy and I, but out of my peripheral vision I saw Harvey get up. He took huge strides down the bleachers, skipping every other bench. He came right across the floor to where we were and tapped Tommy on the shoulder. "May I cut in?" he asked, just like that. Tommy, who was on the shy side, shrugged and stepped aside.

Harvey pulled me so close our whole bodies touched. My head fell sideways against his chest, and I just let it stay there.

That's the way we danced all evening. Not show-offy like before, but like a king and queen among peons. In between dances we kept to ourselves. He didn't seem to have guys he hung around with, and I didn't go back to Denise and the girls.

I still think of that night as a scene out of a movie. Once Mr. Hanson, my biology teacher, came by and took our picture. "He's my favorite teacher," I told Harvey.

"Mine too," he said.

It turned out that we both liked biology. Harvey told me he wanted to be a famous surgeon someday, so famous he could pick and choose his operations. That would leave him plenty of free time for his hobbies, which he said were going to be collecting modern art and raising golden retrievers.

I told him how much I liked biology lab. I said that it didn't bother me at all to pith a frog and that you could tell more about a frog's guts from looking at my drawings than you could tell from looking at a dissected frog.

Harvey laughed, and I could tell he liked the way I had said "frog's guts." He said that I should become a medical illustrator for scientific textbooks and that he might write one someday. I said that was a good idea.

I asked him if he liked art museums, and he said no, not really, but that he loved art. I knew just what he meant. Things like that kept happening. He was easier to talk to than any boy I'd ever known.

Just before the last dance Moose came over and said, "Hey, city slicker, you and your child bride want a ride to Joe's Pizza? Some of the guys and their chicks are going in Ziggy's car."

The words "child bride" embarrassed me.

"Tell you what, Moose," Harvey said in a tone that sounded appreciative but that somehow I knew was put on. "Can I let you know after the dance?"

"Yeah, sure, Harve, take your time, you know what I mean?" Moose's voice was so slack I realized he had been drinking.

"I'll let you know," said Harvey. I could feel him tensing up.

"Well?" he asked as we were dancing.

"I don't know," I said, deciding to tell him the truth. "I mean, I would love to, but I told my mother I was going with my friends to Victor's Palace."

Harvey looked hurt, and I got mad at myself for not starting out quite right. What I should have said was that my mother was strict and that she would never let me go to Joe's, which was a hangout with a reputation in the next town. I should have said that I wasn't even sure that I would *want* to go anywhere with Moose and his friend Ziggy.

"What's the matter with you?" asked Harvey, scowling. "Isn't Moose good enough for you? Or is it me perhaps? Life is too short to be so indecisive." He raised his head and started dancing faster and more fancily than before. It was almost as if he were defying me to stumble. I didn't know what had made him be that way, but I didn't like it so I paid attention. When at the end of the record he dipped me, I was ready. We ended perfectly.

"Harvey," I said. "The reason I didn't say yes was —"

"Too late," he said.

Like perfect strangers, we walked to the cafeteria. "My jacket's down there," I said, pointing to the front.

"Mine's by the windows," he said.

Everything was ending too soon. "Harvey," I said.

"See you 'round, Barnes. Don't burn any down." Without a backward glance Harvey walked away.

· 11 ·

The cafeteria was filled with kids looking for their coats and jackets, most of which had fallen off tables and were getting trampled on the floor. The fluorescent lights gave the room a green noisy look. Half in tears, I went to find Denise.

"I found out that he moved here over the summer from New York City," she said. "What's the matter?"

"He's neat," said Donna, who was under the table. "Where'd he go?"

"He asked me to go to Joe's Pizza with him and some other upperclassmen, and when I said no, he got upset."

"Maybe he thought you didn't like him," said Ginger.

"I *danced* with him all night." Agitated as I was, I couldn't help savoring the words "upperclassmen" and "danced with him all night." My friends were looking at me the way they usually look at Clearlight.

"Boys are insecure," said Denise. "You have to spell it out for them. Right, Clearlight?"

Clearlight just came over. "Right, what?" Her black parka with the purple lining was over her shoulders. "So who was that guy, Lisa?"

"Harvey Burns," said Denise. "He moved here from New York over the summer. He got mad at Lisa when she said she wouldn't go to Joe's with him. I said he must be insecure."

Clearlight looked at me and snapped her gum. "Joe's is the pits," she said.

"I know," I said.

"If you care for him, let him know. Go get him."

"Go get him?"

"Love is a function of communication," said Clearlight, putting her arms into her jacket sleeves. As the purple lining flashed around her head, she looked like a model in *Vogue*. We all just stood there and watched.

"She means get him to walk you home," said Donna, breaking the spell. "Denise will tell her mother. Mrs. Hall will understand."

"You really think I should?"

"You're the one who has to choose," said Clearlight, snapping her gum. "Rick is walking me."

"Look," said Denise excitedly, pointing. "There he is! Go on!"

I saw him, looked back into Denise's eager eyes for a second, grabbed my jacket, and ran down the aisle between the tables.

Harvey was standing outside with his collar up and his hands pushed down in his pockets. He was talking to Moose. Well, that settled that. I wasn't going over there now. Then Moose saw me.

"Hey, Harve," he bellowed. "There's your little chickadee!"

I thought I would die.

"Don't be a chicken with your chickadee, Harve!" yelled Moose. He put both his hands on Harvey's back and pushed him right up against me. The other boys roared with laughter.

For a split second Harvey looked at me; then he spun around and walked right up to Moose with his hands still in his pockets. "Don't call me chicken, and don't ever push me again. You hear that, Dubinsky?"

One of the boys behind Moose yelled, "Another fight! All right!" But Moose was grinning.

"Hey, Harve buddy," he said drunkenly, "no offense. I was just trying to be, you know, like a little lovebird." Moose flapped his arms up and down and said, "Tweet, tweet," in a high, silly voice.

Harvey shook his head and started to turn toward me when Moose yelled, "What *did* you quit the team for anyway, Burns? You were a pretty good kiker, I mean, kicker!"

Harvey turned and ran for Moose, but

Moose was too drunk to fight. He just grabbed Harvey and laughed hysterically. "Only kidding, Harvey. Ah-ha-ha-ha! But seriously, why did you quit?" Tears of laughter were running down Moose's stupid face.

Harvey flung Moose's arm off his shoulder. I couldn't stand watching them anymore. Without even thinking, I ran up to Harvey and pulled him toward me as if I had something urgent to tell him. He let me pull him away, and when we reached the top of the walkway down to Hill Street, he stopped for a second, shrugged, and grinned as if everything was fine.

"My friends said I should have asked you to walk me home," I said.

"They were right," he said, putting his arm through mine.

· 12 ·

When we reached the construction site for the new senior citizens' home, I told Harvey that there were two places to cut across, a steep part and a long path, and that we were standing by the steep part.

"Come on," said Harvey. He grabbed my hand and jumped down the bank. Before I knew it, we were running, slipping, sliding so fast we almost toppled over head-first. Then we were at the bottom, slowing down on level land.

The dug-up field was gray in the moonlight, with dark construction equipment casting eerie black designs on the hard dirt ground. Just a few minutes before we had been in a noisy cafeteria filled with kids and light. Now we were alone, catching our breath in the middle of a broken up field. Harvey was still holding my hand.

"When I was little, this used to be a trailer park," I said. "We used to go trick-or-treating here because the people in the trailers gave out big candy bars. They didn't want us to think they were poor."

"You think about things like that?" asked Harvey.

I didn't know what to say, so I said, "I don't know."

There was a long silence. I used Harvey's hand for balance as I reached down with my other hand and dumped dirt out of my flats. "Where did you go trick-or-treating in New York?" I asked to make conversation.

Harvey looked at me aghast. "How would I know? My father's name used to be Bernstein."

"What?"

"I'm Jewish. Didn't you know that?

"I don't understand," I said, confused. "Don't Jewish people celebrate Halloween?" I tried to think quickly. No, I hadn't known he was Jewish. I hadn't thought about religion. Most of the Jewish kids, like Ellen Goldberg, lived on the other side of town, but some lived near me. They went out on Halloween, didn't they? But wasn't there another name for Halloween? All Hallows'

Eve? It did sound sort of holy. How stupid could I be?

When I looked up to apologize, Harvey burst into laughter. "You know what you are? Gullible. You probably don't even know what a kike is. You probably didn't even know Moose was insulting me."

I shook my head in confusion. Harvey laughed even harder, and moonlight bounced off his braces.

"I don't know why you're laughing," I said.

Harvey dropped my hand and ran over to one of the bulldozers. "Let's climb up!" he shouted.

It was absurd, but there was nothing else to do, so I went around to the other side and climbed up. It wasn't easy. Harvey had has hands on two levers that stuck out from the instrument panel and was pretending to drive, making rumbling motor and screeching brake sounds like a little boy. I had to laugh, but I felt uncomfortable.

"Harvey, stop! People might hear you!"

But he didn't stop. He just got louder and more mirthless.

"They'll think your crazy!" I said.

Harvey shoved his hands in his pockets. "What do you mean they'll think I'm crazy?"

"You're not supposed to do that."

"You mean the Polacks in Bar Ferry don't do this?"

I thought he was teasing me again, so I

laughed. But he didn't laugh back. What a puzzle Harvey was. One minute he was so much fun; the next minute he acted as if I were some kind of enemy. It had been the same on the dance floor. I wondered if I should be afraid to be alone with him, but for some reason I didn't feel afraid.

"How do you know so much about bulldozers?" I finally asked.

"Magazines. I get lots of magazines."

"Do you get *Natural History* magazine? Mr. Hanson told me it was good."

"Yeah, I get that. You can have my old copies if you want."

"Thank you," I said. And then because I realized I didn't feel the slightest bit afraid, I asked, "What's the matter, Harvey? Don't you like Bar Ferry?"

"Bar Ferry?" He thought about the question and shrugged. "It's different, if you know what I mean. No offense."

"No."

Harvey shrugged again. His jacket made dry, crunchy sounds. "It's hard to explain. Let me put it this way. I like the swans better than the people."

"I love the swans!" I said. It was true. I often went to our town dock to feed them. They were new to Bar Ferry this year. No one knew where they had come from or why they had never come before. There were seven of them, and I had given a secret name to each one.

"Where'd you learn to dance?" Harvey asked.

"My father. It sounds weird, but there used to be a piano in our dining room. My mother used to play songs from shows we'd seen on Broadway. My father and I would waltz around the dining room table, just barely making it past the china cabinet. 'Careful,' my mother would yell, 'or you'll break the glasses!' but she'd keep on playing, and we'd keep on dancing 'round and 'round."

"Charming," said Harvey. "Quaint. Tell me more about your family."

At first I thought he was being sarcastic, but when I looked into his eyes, I saw he was sincere, so I continued. "Every summer we used to travel, mostly around New England, but once we went all the way to California and back. We camped out in state parks every night."

Harvey was quiet. Then he asked, "Lisa, are they dead?"

"Who?"

"Your parents. You keep saying 'used to.' "

"God, no. It's just that we don't do those things anymore. It's as if we ran out of energy. We don't do anything together anymore."

"Parents are weird," said Harvey. "They're very changeable. Have you ever noticed that? One day they're one thing, and the next day they're another. And you have to go along with it just because you're their kid."

"I know," I said. "Believe me, I know. My parents used to have fun. Then somehow we changed from a noisy family to a quiet family." I laughed a small, embarrassed laugh and told Harvey something I had never told anyone. "My father sleeps in the guest room now. He says it's because the bed there is better for his back. How dumb does he think I am?"

Now Harvey knew my worst secret. I wondered if I had gone too far. "It's not really a big deal, though," I added.

"Do you think they'll get divorced?" asked Harvey softly.

I put my head down. "I don't know," I whispered, shaking my head. "Let's change the subject."

Harvey shifted position in his seat. "Well," he said, staring straight into the darkness, "my parents sleep in the same bed, but that doesn't mean they're happy. My father drives my mother crazy. He drives me insane too. He's a fanatic . . . oh, forget it, I can't explain it. And besides, who cares, right? Sitting here like this? Why should we talk about parents? Let's make them disappear." Harvey waved his hand in the air. "Poof. They're gone. What a relief."

I smiled to myself. I was glad I had confided in him.

· 13 ·

The night seemed to get darker and quieter. Beauty, Brighty, Beast, and Bay; Kathy,

Darling, and Café. Those were my names for the swans. I felt like telling them to Harvey just to see what he'd say. I didn't think he would laugh at me.

Just as I looked up, he reached over and put his hand on the back of my head. *"Tes cheveux brillent au clair de lune,"* he said.

Something like a shooting star went through my stomach. "I take Spanish," I whispered.

"I said, 'Your hair is shining in the moonlight.'"

"It is?" I asked. After all I had gone through earlier that day with my hair, I could hardly believe that I was now sitting in a bulldozer with a boy I never knew before, in whom I had just confided my worst secret, and that he was speaking to me in French and telling me that he actually liked my hair.

"Let's get out of here," said Harvey abruptly. He jumped down from the bulldozer and started jogging toward Prince Street.

"That's not the way!" I yelled. I scrambled down and caught up with him. "I live that way!" I pointed toward Rivergate Homes.

Harvey changed directions but was still going so fast I could hardly keep up with him. In no time we had crossed the street in front of the two cement pillars that framed the entrance to my development.

"Why does one have his mouth open and the other have his mouth closed?" asked

Harvey, offhand, as if he hadn't just been so romantic.

He was referring to the two big fish that were cast into the cement. To tell the truth, I had never noticed before, but there in the lamplight I could see he was right. One fish had its mouth open, and the other didn't.

"Who knows?" I said. I started quickly into Rivergate, thinking this time *I* would set the pace, but then I slowed down because Harvey was walking slowly and studying the homes, probably noticing right away that each house was one of three basic designs. I had hoped he *wouldn't* notice that.

"How do you ever find your way around here?" he finally asked after I had led the way around several curves that were supposed to make the layout of the development interesting.

"Easy," I said. We were on my street, and I was wondering what in the world was going to happen next. Harvey was a little rude. Still, I liked the feeling of walking down my street in the dark next to him, and for our time on the dance floor and that brief moment in the bulldozer I had no regrets. We walked up my front walk, which, like every third house, was laid out in an S curve. I stepped onto the first step and turned around to face him.

"That was great, you know, us, dancing."

Harvey looked straight into my eyes, which were now on his level, and didn't say anything. He seemed very serious, as if he were considering something profound.

"I had a pretty good time," I added.

Harvey shrugged. He rocked back on his heels and said, "Maybe when I get my car, I'll take you for a ride."

"You're getting a car?"

"Sure," he said. "In a couple of weeks. It's a present for getting my braces off."

I wondered how he'd look without his braces and had to put my head down so he wouldn't see me smile. Really handsome, I knew. His loafers were so polished they gleamed in the moonlight.

Harvey touched my chin and tipped my head up. I shut my eyes, and he kissed me very lightly on the lips.

"Maybe then, Lisa Barnes," he said quietly with his face still close to mine, "maybe then I'll give you a real kiss."

· 14 ·

I shut the door behind me and leaned back against it in the dark. I was flabbergasted. I felt as if I had just been kissed by the most amazing sixteen-year-old boy in Bar Ferry, if not in all New York State, if not in all America, if not in all the world.

"That wasn't Mrs. Hall," said my mother from the living room. I heard her straighten up in the Barcalounger. She came over and snapped on the hall light. "Was it." This was a statement, not a question.

I took a deep breath and wrapped my arms around my ribs so I wouldn't collapse.

"Well?"

"It was just a boy. It's nothing," I said.

"Just a boy is not nothing to me," she said. "You told me you were going to be driven by Mrs. Hall. What happened to Victor's Palace? Don't tell me Mrs. Hall backed out on one of her commitments."

I held my face stone still so she wouldn't see how upset she was making me, but I guess I must have sighed because suddenly she said, "Don't sigh at me, young lady."

"His name is Harvey Burns," I managed to say. "I met him at the dance. He asked if he could walk me home." Inside I twinged at the slight lie, but no way was I going to tell her I actually asked him. "Denise said her mother would understand."

"So is that who you answer to these days? Denise's mother?"

I didn't speak.

"Next thing I know Mrs. Hall will be taking you and Denise to a clinic for birth control pills."

"Mother!"

"Don't 'Mother' me. Why didn't you call?"

"Next time I will."

"Well, to make sure you remember that, you're grounded this weekend."

"You mean I can't even go over to Denise's or Clearlight's?" I realized the whole time I was with Harvey, a part of my mind was imagining telling the girls about him later on.

My father came upstairs from the basement, carrying a roll of blueprints. "I think I've got it!" he said enthusiastically. He tapped me on the head with the blueprints, then looked at me and my mother. "What's going on here?"

"Lisa was walked home by a boy," said my mother.

My father smiled. "So you had a good time after all."

"She's grounded for the weekend," said my mother, "because she didn't call to tell us the change in plans. As far as we knew, Mrs. Hall was bringing her to Victor's Palace and then home."

"I see," said my father. He tried to look stern too, and then, hoping the subject was over and eager to share what was on his mind, blurted out, "Does anyone want to see my plans for a completely solar house?"

"Not now, Bill," said my mother, exasperated.

"It's ninety percent underground," he said proudly.

"Maybe tomorrow, Dad," I said, starting up the stairs. It was strange the way alliances in our family could shift. One minute my mother and father would side against me, another minute my father and I would side against her, and sometimes, like now, my mother and I, usually at war with each other, would hit upon an unexpected truce as we both tried to avoid my father. We were like nations at the UN.

· 15 ·

There was a tap on the door.

"Lisa, are you awake?" I heard my mother ask.

I was awake, but I didn't answer. I heard the door open slightly.

"Let her sleep," I heard my father whisper.

"But I want her to help me clean the attic."

"Let's go out first. I'll let you off at Shoprite, go look at the VW, and pick you up on my way back. Let her sleep until we get back."

"You indulge her too much."

"Oh, Heather."

"Well, you do."

I kept my eyes closed, waiting for them to leave. Finally I heard them shut my door and go downstairs. At last the house was quiet. Turning over, I made myself comfortable and went over every detail from the night before. Harvey Burns had picked *me* out of a crowd, had danced with *me* as he had danced with no other, had walked *me* home, and had kissed *me. Me!* It was true that at times he acted peculiar, but that must have been, as Denise would say, a boy's natural insecurity.

The point was that right at this very moment in Bar Ferry was a boy who liked *me*.

And he was a tall, handsome, and intelligent boy, more interesting than any other boy I knew. The more I thought about it, the more I came to the conclusion that I had fallen in love for the first time in my life. Holding my pillow in my arms, I fell back asleep.

Honk! Honk!

The second I heard my father's car, I awoke, flew out of bed, threw on my jeans and a red flannel shirt, ran downstairs, grabbed a piece of bread, poured a glass of milk, and sat down at the kitchen table, trying to look as if I had been up for a while.

My parents came in, each carrying two bags.

"Let me help," I said, taking one from my mother.

"Don't take this one," she said. "Get the others in the car."

"What are all these apples for?" I asked, returning with a bushel basket full of them.

"Got them over in Fairley," said my father. "A great deal. I thought you and I could make some applesauce."

"Lisa's going to help me clean the attic," said my mother.

"You said in the car you were going to do that after lunch."

"Well?"

"Well, then we can make applesauce this morning, right, Lisa?" He smiled at me conspiratorially.

I don't know how he expected me to smile back at him. Did he think I liked having my day planned like that? I knew I was grounded, but I didn't think I'd been sentenced to work camp.

The phone rang. Harvey! I couldn't believe he'd call this soon! Since I was nearest to the phone, I reached out calmly and picked up the receiver.

"Hello?"

"Hi-ii." It was Denise. Only she said "Hi" in two syllables.

"Hi," I said. "Just a second." I looked at my parents and said, "It's for me." They looked at each other, readjusting alliances, and then started unpacking groceries. Normally I would have gone upstairs to the phone in my mother's room and asked them to hang up downstairs, but that didn't seem wise under the present circumstances.

"I bet you hoped it was Harvey," said Denise.

"Not really," I said, trying to sound a little bored.

"Why? Did he already call?"

"Not really," I said again.

"Mmm-m," said Denise. Then she paused. "Well, I found out all about him." I knew she would string it out forever, but I wasn't going to ask what she had found out. Finally she said, "Aren't you even interested?"

"Sure."

"He's Jewish."

"I know that," I said, surprised and annoyed that it was the first thing she said. "So?"

"My mother says his house probably costs two hundred thousand dollars. We got the address from Information and rode by it."

"You what?"

"Mom says those Jewish people really know how to make money."

"Denise," I said disapprovingly. My mother looked up from the wax paper drawer. Now she knew whom I was talking to.

"What's wrong with saying that, Lisa? It's a compliment. Listen. You know how on Ridgewood Drive they don't have house numbers? Well, a mailbox said 'Burns' so that's how we knew where he lived. My mother put it all together. You know the construction going on at the old train station? It's being done by people named Burns! His mother and father are opening something there."

"They are?"

"Didn't he tell you *anything*?"

"No, I mean, yes. Plenty."

"Can you come over? We want to hear all about it!"

"No."

"You can't?"

"Not this weekend."

My mother walked back to get another full bag. By the satisfied look on her face I swear she knew Denise had just asked me over.

"What do you mean, not this weekend?"

"Mm-m-m."

"Can't talk?"

"Right."

"Oh."

"Mm-m-m."

"Did you get in trouble last night?"

"Mm-hmm."

"Why? Did you come home real late?"

I sighed.

"Oh, brother." I could tell Denise was imagining much more than what had actually gone on.

I laughed.

"So you have to stay in *all* weekend?"

"Right," I said, enjoying the envy in Denise's voice. I could just imagine what she would tell her mother.

· 16 ·

My father set up an apple-paring gadget he had sent for from a company in Vermont, but it didn't work. Finally we just did the apples by hand. I had my method and he had his. My method was to start at the top with a paring knife and go around and around, unwinding the peel like a green and white ribbon, as long as I could make it. His method was to quarter the apples with a small sharp knife, slice away the core side, and peel away the skin side. Without saying so, we raced to see whose method was faster.

Eventually my father put a bowl of peeled and sliced apples in a big pot on the stove.

"I wonder when you put in the sugar," he said.

"I don't know," I said.

He looked it up in *The Joy of Cooking*.

"After," he said. "And there's no need to

make it too sweet. There's too much sugar in things these days."

"I guess so," I said. I wondered what a sophisticated boy like Harvey was doing right now. I was pretty sure he wasn't making applesauce. He might still be in bed, thinking about me.

"What are you smiling at?"

"Nothing."

"I suppose you think it's silly making applesauce when you can go out and buy it so easily. I suppose you might even think it's silly for your *father* to make applesauce."

"No," I said. I couldn't stop smiling, though.

"Tell the truth, I'd like to put up a lot of food for the winter. That solar house I was telling you about? I'm building it for Mr. Murphy, but I wouldn't mind building it somewhere upstate for us. We could raise our own food, live free from dependence on Arab oil, and be safe from nuclear attack."

"There's no place safe from nuclear attack," I said. "We studied it at school."

"Oh?"

"We had a speaker from Civil Defense. He said his job was a joke. Nuclear bomb shelters will turn into crematoriums, and evacuation plans won't work. The radiation will get everyone in the end."

My father stirred the apples thoughtfully. "I suppose you're right," he finally said. I could tell that he didn't agree but he was glad we were having a discussion. He sighed and said, "I don't know what kind of world we're handing you kids."

I had reached the top of another bowl of sliced apples, so I brought it over to him and dumped it in the pot.

He squinted his eyes and asked, "You and your friends, Lisa — do you think about . . . do you feel anxious about the threat of nuclear attack?"

"Not really," I said.

"Well, what do you kids talk about when you're together?"

"I don't know." My father was beginning to sound like a guidance counselor. He knew a boy had walked me home last night. So why, if he wanted to get close to me, didn't he ask me about that? It was impossible for me to bring Harvey up now. I mean, how would it look to shift the conversation from nuclear holocaust to Harvey? Pretty stupid.

I glanced at the phone and had the distinct sensation that at that very moment Harvey had glanced at his phone too and was thinking about me. I had never had ESP so strongly before. It made the hair on my arms stand up. I almost picked up the receiver to see if he was there.

My father trickled sugar from the sugar bag into the pot. He poured, stirred, tasted, added some more sugar, stirred, tasted, and went on like that for a long time. We didn't talk anymore. He was thinking about applesauce, and I was thinking about Harvey. Without my mother around we were both fairly relaxed. Outside, it began to rain thick, noisy drops.

"You had a pretty good time last night?" My father asked suddenly, out of the blue.

"Mm-hmm."

"A boy walked you home?"

"Mm-hmm." "Daddy," I wanted to say, "remember how we used to dance around the dining room table? Well, the boy who walked me home can dance like that. Kids cleared the floor and watched us, and afterward they clapped."

"I remember the first time I walked a girl home. Her name was Hester."

My father was stirring and staring peacefully at the exhaust fan. There was a coziness in our kitchen right then, and a potential for something hung in the air. My father took the pot of applesauce off the stove and set it on the counter. Maybe he would tell me all about Hester, and I would tell him all about Harvey. But just then the phone rang. Harvey! Inside I jumped, but outside I calmly extended my arm and lifted the receiver.

"No, thank you. We don't want any," said my mother. She had already picked up upstairs, and as I listened I heard her hang up. I put the receiver back on the hook.

"Who was that?"

"Some salesman. Mom answered."

"Oh. Taste this. See what you think."

Without thinking I swallowed the spoonful of applesauce he held out and burned my whole throat. Quickly I drank some cold water. "It was much too hot!" I said angrily.

"I'm sorry. I just meant for you to taste it. I think it's sweet enough.

"Well, fine then." I don't know why I was so angry at him. He hadn't meant to burn me, and he couldn't help it if Harvey hadn't called.

"I guess we'll freeze it," he said, taking down plastic containers from a top shelf. I could tell he had forgotten all about Hester. "If we moved upstate, we might not have a freezer, so we'd have to can it, but for now I don't see why we can't just freeze it."

"Oh, can the whole subject," I felt like saying. "God knows, there's more important things in life than applesauce!"

· 17 ·

I went upstairs, lay down exhausted on my bed, and listened to my mother moving boxes around over my head in the attic. I knew she had started up there ahead of time just to make me and my father feel guilty, but I didn't care. I had begun to develop a bad case of phone-on-the-brain, so bad I tiptoed into my mother's room and looked up Harvey's number in the phone book. It wasn't there. Then I remembered that Denise had said he lived on Ridgewood Drive, so I quietly dialed the operator.

"That number is 555-4739. Have a good day," she said.

I wrote the number down on my pad but

didn't make the call because I heard mother starting down the attic stairs, which opened into my room. I ran back into my room and composed myself, drawing a horse on my pad while covering Harvey's number with my elbow so she wouldn't see it.

My mother was carrying old dresses and coats over her arms, so many she could hardly fit through the door.

"Let me help you," I said, getting up.

"Take these downstairs to the couch and come back for more, if you're not too busy," she said, glancing suspiciously at my sketchbook.

Upstairs in the chilly attic we faced each other under the bare light bulb. "Empty the drawers of the old brown bureau," she said.

I went over and opened the bottom drawer.

"What are you staring at?" asked my mother.

"Old wallpaper," I said.

My mother came over and stood next to me. Then she knelt down beside me, her jeans right next to mine. We both stared at the wallpaper. I reached in and unrolled part of the hummingbirds that used to be in the dining room, and she reached in and unrolled part of the ivy that used to be in the kitchen. The wallpaper we now had in both rooms was beige with a thin white stripe.

"They were pretty, weren't they?" she said in a surprisingly soft tone of voice.

"I could draw those hummingbirds by heart," I said. "And the ivy reminds me of

Christmas cookies. I used to snitch pieces of gingerbread dough and eat it with my head turned to the wall so you wouldn't see me. I pretended I was studying the leaves."

My mother unrolled the ivy a little more. "Lisa," she began thoughtfully. "It's not that I didn't want you to have a good time at the dance last night. It's just that I *have* to be able to trust you. I'm very busy, and I have a lot on my mind. I can't watch your every step. If we're going to be friends, you're going to have to come home when I expect you and by whatever method of transportation we have previously agreed upon."

"But, Mom, you don't understand. Some kids asked Harvey and me to go in a car with them to Joe's Pizza. I said no because I knew you wouldn't let me. I was trying to do what I thought was right."

"What would have been right," my mother said slowly and deliberately, "would have been to come home with Mrs. Hall, as we had discussed."

"But, Mom —"

"No buts about it." My mother rolled up the ivy paper briskly and tapped the roll against her palm for emphasis. "What *you* don't understand, Lisa, is that in addition to working nine to five every day, I have to carry in my head all the responsibilities of this household. It's all on me, and if it makes me crabby sometimes, well, all I can say is I'm sorry."

If my mother's words were meant to make me feel better, they didn't work. I snapped back the end of the hummingbirds and lifted up an armful of wallpaper rolls. "So you want to throw these out?" I stood and held them in my arms like a baby.

My mother clicked her tongue. "I *had* planned to put the summer blankets in here."

"Then where should I put these? In the garbage?"

My mother sighed and stood up. "I'll get a Hefty bag," she said.

I think we both felt terrible to see the hummingbirds and the ivy disappear into the big brown plastic bag, but we said no more about it. I closed the bag tightly with a twist tie and carried it down to the trash pile on the sidewalk.

That night my parents went out to a movie. They said I could go with them, but I didn't want to be with either of them, and I *did* want to be home in case Harvey called. I watched an old movie called *Badlands* on TV. It wasn't that old really, maybe ten years. Martin Sheen played a teenager who went around killing people who got in his way. Sissy Spacek was his girl friend. It was good.

Twice during commercial breaks I dialed Harvey's number, not really to talk to him but just to hear what the background noises were like in his home. I planned to listen for a few seconds, then hang up. But no one answered. I figured Harvey and his parents had gone into the city to visit old friends or maybe see a Broadway show.

· 18 ·

All day Sunday it rained cats and dogs. Denise called to say she and Clearlight were going to the mall.

"Did you-know-who call?" she asked.

"He went into the city with his family," I said. "They probably got tickets to something."

Denise gave a little sniff, which meant she had a question on her mind. "Do you ever wonder," she said, "no, never mind, I shouldn't ask."

I held the receiver away from me, looked at the earpiece, and gave it the finger. I put it back to my ear.

"Ask what?" I said, very ho-hum.

"No, it's silly."

"Now that you started, you may as well finish."

"Well, I was thinking, I was wondering, do you think, I mean, well, let's say you and Harvey become a real couple. You know. Could you picture, you know . . ."

"What?"

"You know, that he might be The One?"

She was referring to Clearlight's theory, which she had told us one night in Donna's basement, about the difference between a boyfriend and The One. All the lights had been turned out except the aquarium lights behind the bar. Clearlight was sitting on a barstool, and the rest of us were sitting on the floor. We were supposed to take turns being the Adviser, but no one except Clearlight ever wanted a turn.

I forget what the question was, but Clearlight's answer became a classic in our minds. There is a difference, she said, between a boyfriend and The One. A boyfriend is someone you really like. You may even love him. But that does not make him The One. The One is the *first* person you let make love to you. Clearlight was emphatic about the matter of choice. She said if you didn't choose from the depths of your heart who The One was going to be, then your first time would be with just anyone, a tragedy you could never erase from your mind.

Denise had asked Clearlight how you know who The One is, and Clearlight had replied, "You just know."

You just know. Here I was in my mother's room, sitting on the edge of the bed that used to be my father's. It was not a good place for me to talk about sex.

"Give me a break, Denise," I said.

"I knew I shouldn't have asked that."

"It's okay."

"You sure you aren't mad?"

"No."

"Okay."

"I'll see you tomorrow."

"Okay. Bye."

I went into my room and drew a sketch of Harvey and me dancing. Then I wrote "Mr.

and Mrs. H. Burns" under it, tore it up into confetti, and dumped it in the wastebasket.

I took my pad into my mother's bedroom and dialed 555-4739. I knew the number by heart. I figured that by now the Burnses would be back from the city. It was almost five. But they weren't home yet. I let the phone ring anyway because I liked the idea that I was making a sound ring in Harvey's house even if there was no one there to hear it.

"Hello?"

My heart stopped.

"Hello? Hello?" It was a man's voice. He sounded annoyed. I couldn't hang up.

"Who is this? Who is this calling our house? Hang up or I'll call the police!"

I hung up and held my hand over my heart. I should never have done that. It must have been Harvey's father. If he told Harvey about the phone call, Harvey would know it was me. What a jerk he would think I was! He would hate me. My mother and father were coming upstairs. I practically ran into them in the hall.

"What are you doing?" asked my mother.

"Nothing," I said, my heart pounding.

I saw her give my father a look. I shut my door with a slam and threw myself on my bed.

· 19 ·

Monday morning Harvey's bulldozer didn't look so big in the daylight. I'd hoped I would see him before school, but now it was probably too late.

That was another thing about my parents. They both left the house before me in the morning, so it was up to me to be on time. Denise's mother made Denise eggs every morning and drove her to school. They would have picked me up too, but I could never get ready in time. Not that I wanted eggs either, I can't stand them, but it was hard to have to do everything in the morning myself. I had already been late so many times the guidance counselor, Mrs. Beauchamp, had called me to see her. She was pretty nice actually. She said since my grades so far were good, all she was going to do was warn me. I got the feeling she personally didn't see what the big deal was, being late five or ten minutes some mornings. She was just doing her job.

The first bell rang as I ran down the hall. Kids were crowding the halls, on their way to classes, entering doors. I had only two minutes to get to my class, which was on the other side of the building. Harvey would surely be in his classroom by now. I wondered where it was, when I would see him, *if* I would see him, what he would say, and what I would say back.

And then there he was. I saw him, leaning against my locker, watching everyone walk by as if he hadn't a care in the world. He wasn't even looking down the hall to see if I was coming. He didn't seem to mind that he wasn't on his way somewhere. He had on a black turtleneck sweater and tan corduroy jeans. I slowed down and got right up next to him before he finally turned and noticed me.

"Hi," I said.

"Hi."

"I'm late."

He shrugged and moved away from my locker. He watched as I did my combination. It didn't click. I did it again. It didn't click again.

"Stop watching me!" I said with a nervous laugh.

"What's your combination?" he asked.

You weren't supposed to tell anyone. "Thirty-two right, fourteen left, two right," I said.

He shifted his books to his left hand and did my door with his right: 32 right, 14 left, 2 right. The lock clicked. I opened the door, threw in my jacket, and grabbed some books as the second bell rang.

"I'm really late," I said looking at him apologetically so he wouldn't think I was trying to get rid of him, yet walking as fast as I could down the hall.

Harvey kept up without effort.

"Where's your first class?" I asked.

"Back there." Harvey gestured with his head.

"Aren't you going to be late?"

"Probably. What are all those books for?"

"Biology," I said. "Extra credit. I'm doing a series of sketches on chick embryology."

Harvey nodded. I liked that. Denise would have said, "Brownie points, Brownie points."

The third bell rang. "Now we're both late," I said.

"See you," Harvey said. He gave me a wink as he turned.

I didn't see him again until lunch. Sophomores ate at 11:45. Juniors ate at noon. In the cafeteria I sat across from Denise and Donna so I could see the door.

"Has he come in yet?" asked Denise.

"Not yet," I said.

"I saw him Saturday night at Record World," said Donna.

"I thought you said he went into the city," Denise said to me.

"I thought they did," I said, exasperated but trying not to show it. "Maybe they went Sunday. All I know is he met me at my locker this morning and walked me to class even though it made him late."

"I hear his house cost two hundred and fifty thousand dollars," said Donna.

Tommy, Bobby, and some of the other tenth-grade boys were doing something in the middle of their table, which was right next to ours. They kept sneaking looks over at us and laughing hysterically.

Denise glanced their way.

"Ignore them, Denise," I said. On my plate was barbecue beef on a bun, creamed corn, and three pineapple rings. The three different juices were running together. Reluctantly I took a small bite of pineapple.

The boys were egging on Bobby to do something. Laughing so hard he could hardly walk, he came over and put his barbecue beef down in front of Denise.

"For you, madame," he said, beet red. Then he ran back to his table and collapsed.

"We dare you to eat it!" yelled Tommy. All the boys were watching.

Denise looked at the plate, at the boys, then back to her plate. She giggled. "Sure," she said with a toss of her head. "I'll eat it."

"Denise!" I hissed. "Don't!"

"Eat it, eat it!" shouted the boys.

Upperclassmen were starting to come in as Denise took her first bite. The boys were making so much noise that an aide had to come over. I put my hand up to hide my face.

"This is mortifying," I said.

"I bet they spit in it," said Donna.

"Bobby wouldn't do that," said Denise. "Anyway, I'm full. I'm not going to eat any more."

I was too embarrassed to watch for Harvey, so I didn't see where he was sitting. When it came time for our section to leave, I didn't want him to think I was snubbing him, so I glanced up at the clock, sweeping across all the juniors with my eyes. There he was, sitting next to Ellen Goldberg. She was leaning her shoulder against his, smiling as if he had just said something very amusing. Instantly I understood that Ellen had a competitive edge on me. I could dance, but she was Jewish. And for Harvey, for some reason, that was important.

· 20 ·

The day, which had started out bad (I was late) and had turned good (Harvey was waiting for me at my locker), seemed to have turned bad permanently. In home ec Mrs. Jennings sprang a surprise quiz on us. I had completely forgotten we were supposed to memorize the characteristics of cheese over the weekend. The test had ten cheeses in a column on the left and eleven phrases in a column on the right.

I connected Swiss with "firm, slightly nutty" and Cheddar with "crumbly, range of sharpness," but that was all I knew. There were eight more cheeses, all foreign. I would get a 20. Denise, Tommy, and Bobby, I noticed, were busy connecting one pair after another. It didn't seem fair that kids who thought spitburger was funny would get a better mark in cooking than me, the only one who had to cook at home.

Home ec was a ridiculous class. Every tenth-grader had to take it. Really. What a waste. I knew Harvey would feel the same disgust for it that I did.

My bad luck streak continued into gym. Certain athletic girls, juniors and seniors, can get out of study hall to help the gym teachers. They are called girls' leaders. Guess who the girls' leader was in my class? Ellen Goldberg.

And there she was, a foot away, standing in her mint green satin bra, twirling the key to the locker room, and asking me, as I was pulling off my sweater, about Harvey.

I grabbed my gym suit and held it up in front of me, putting my hand over the little gold safety pin that held my white bra together.

"I said, what do you think of Harvey Burns?"

I shrugged noncommittally.

"I hear he walked you home Friday night."

"So?"

"You like him?"

"He's okay."

"My cousin goes to Horace Mann, where he used to go. She says he was a nobody there."

"I'm not surprised," I said offhandedly, but actually inside I was.

"Okay, you girls, get a move on!" Ellen yelled. She blew her whistle and walked off. Her underpants were mint green, too.

We were lying on our backs, holding our feet, pointed, six inches off the floor. Mrs. Morrison started counting. I was determined to hold my legs up longer than anyone else. At sixty I thought I would croak. Most of the kids had dropped theirs, but I could see Ellen's down at the end of the row. I knew they were hers because she had little pink pompons on her gym shoes.

My stomach muscles felt as if they were

going to rip apart. Seventy, seventy-one. I tried not to think of the pain. I thought about Harvey sitting next to Ellen in the cafeteria and couldn't stand it any longer. I dropped my legs.

One second later Ellen dropped hers.

"Ellen Goldberg, number one," said Mrs. Morrison.

After school Number Two lingered by her locker, but Harvey didn't show up. Tommy passed by to ask about the new home ec assignment. After the cheese quiz he had been excused from class to help the track coach do something.

"Bring in a cheese recipe," I said tersely because I was mad at his juvenile behavior at lunchtime and because I didn't want him hanging around when Harvey came by.

"What kind of cheese recipe?" he asked.

"What do you mean what kind of cheese recipe? A cheese recipe."

"You mean, like cheese dip?"

"A main-course recipe. We're going to vote on which one to make in class."

"I never heard of a cheese recipe for a main course," said Tommy.

"Didn't you ever hear of macaroni and cheese or cheese soufflé or quiche Lorraine?" I asked impatiently.

"Oh, yeah," said Tommy. He smiled shyly, and I had the feeling he was trying to make up for the foolishness at lunch. "Now I know what you mean."

"See this book?" I said holding up one of the biology books I got from the library. "I'm doing extra credit in chick embryology. I have to go see Mr. Hanson now."

Tommy shook his head in exaggerated wonderment. "I always said you were a brain, Lisa."

"I am not," I said huffily.

"Well, I'll see you around," he said, and he smiled at me again. He walked off one way, and I walked off the other. Except for the two of us, the hall was empty. I thought of the word "irony," which we had been discussing in English class. Some kids just didn't understand what "ironic" meant, but I found it easy to understand. "It is ironic," I could have told them, "that just when a boy I wanted to like me *last* year starts to like me *this* year, I am interested in someone else. Timing and boys," I could have said, "can be extremely ironic."

· 21 ·

The minute I entered Mr. Hanson's room, I saw Harvey and Mr. Hanson walk out of the lab supply room.

"Your ears must be burning," said Mr. Hanson.

I reached up to my ears in confusion and almost dropped my books.

"No, no, I mean we were just talking about you," said Mr. Hanson. "Put your things down and come here a minute. I want to show you something."

I followed them back into the supply room without looking at Harvey. Mr. Hanson stopped in front of a big cardboard box on the counter.

"Oh, my God," I said. Inside was a dead dog.

"It was killed on the road this morning," said Mr. Hanson. "Right in front of me. I stopped to see if I could help. There was no identification on the dog, so the driver didn't know what to do with him. I said I'd put a notice in the paper and take care of the dog myself."

It was a cocker spaniel type of mutt with black blood crusted on its face and chest.

"Poor thing," said Harvey, but he was looking at me. "Mr. Hanson wants me to dissect the dog and rebuild its skeleton for the high school science fair December sixth."

"Ugh," I said, shuddering.

"Look at it this way," said Harvey. He was still looking at me. "It will either become a skeleton in a science show or rot among the worms in the ground. I cut up a fetal pig last year at Horace Mann. It wasn't so bad."

"You'd need some help, Harvey," Mr. Hanson said to him. "But I think you'd have a good entry. I saw a photo in a magazine of some kids who won with a cat skeleton. Three-D projects usually do well. The local winner goes to the county fair in January and possibly the state fair in March. First prize locally is a hundred dollars. County is three hundred, and state is a thousand."

"I'll think it over," said Harvey.

"Are you sure you have the time?" asked Mr. Hanson.

"I'm not going out for sports anymore," said Harvey, picking up his book bag. "Well, Lisa and I had better get going," he said. "We're going down by the river to feed the swans."

I guess I should have hated the way Harvey said that, but if I'm going to tell this story right, I have to admit that sometimes Harvey's bossiness gave me a thrill.

· 22 ·

The streets we walked on sloped down to the river, making it easy for me to keep up with Harvey. I felt pretty relaxed. In the village Harvey turned into the deli to buy a loaf of stale Italian bread.

"You want anything?" he asked me. He had a tan pigskin wallet with four new tens in it.

"No, thank you," I said.

"I'll take a box of powdered doughnuts and two milks," he told the clerk. I wondered if one of the milks was for me.

"White or chocolate?" asked the clerk.

Harvey stared at me. The clerk was looking at me too.

"White," I stammered, furious at my voice for sounding nervous.

It was a cold day, gray as steel and overcast as if it might rain again. All my swans were at the dock. Beauty, Brighty, Beast, and Bay; Kathy, Darling, and Café. This is Harvey. What do you think?

Harvey handed me the bag with the doughnuts and milk and took the loaf of bread for himself. He started tearing off chunks and throwing them to the swans. Beauty and Brighty caught the bread in the air. The others dipped their necks gracefully into the water and came up looking satisfied, all except Café. He wasn't getting any bread.

"Feed the brown one," I said.

"Why?" asked Harvey, deliberately throwing a big chunk to Beast.

"I don't know," I said. "It isn't fair."

"Life isn't fair," said Harvey. He looked at me with his eyebrows raised and his head tipped down like an old preacher. "Didn't your parents ever teach you that, Lisa? Life isn't fair, not for swans or people."

"Or dogs either," I said. I grabbed the bread out of his hands, threw it in the water next to Café, and started running toward the old rock jetty.

"Hey!" yelled Harvey, chasing me.

Wild and giddy, I leaped from rock to rock, my book bag flapping in the air. I could hear Harvey coming after me. The jetty wasn't very long because the end had fallen into the river long ago. When I reached the end, he would have me trapped.

I ran, I got there and stopped. I didn't hear Harvey behind me, probably because I was panting so hard. I stared at the choppy river and the black-green hills on the other side. My breathing calmed down, but I still didn't hear him. Maybe he was sneaking up on me. I crouched down and touched something shiny. Mica, I thought. The shiny bits in the rock are called mica.

Finally, casually, I turned halfway around, reaching for more mica and straining my eyes farther around to see where Harvey was. He was nowhere to be seen. I pretended to finish examining the rock for mica, and then I got up and walked back toward the shore.

Harvey was sitting in a crevice between two big rocks. He had powdered sugar on his lips, and there was only one doughnut left in the box.

"Do you know swans mate for life?" he asked.

"Yes," I said. "I know all about swans. That brown swan will be white next year, just like in 'The Ugly Duckling.'" I jumped down into the crevice and grabbed the last doughnut. I didn't act at all concerned with the phrase "mate for life," but inside I could feel it reverberate in my brain.

Harvey wiped his lips. "You know," he said, "I'm going to need someone to hold the bones while I glue them together."

"You'll probably need someone to make sketches too," I said.

"I could get Ellen Goldberg," he said.

"I was just going to suggest that."

We both started laughing. Then Harvey crushed his milk carton and said, "You and I could win, you know."

"I know," I said, sipping the last bit of my milk.

Harvey smashed the doughnut box in his hands, making confectioners' sugar fly into the air and onto his jacket.

"Harvey!" I yelled, laughing, and would have laughed some more if I hadn't noticed how stormy his face had suddenly become. He almost looked frightened. "What's the matter?" Maybe he thought I was coming on too strong. I sat back against a rock and tried to look low-key.

"Nothing's the matter," he said. Out of the corner of my eyes I saw him slowly put the crushed milk carton and doughnut box into the paper bag. He held the bag thoughtfully between both hands and said, "We could do it at my house."

"Why not at school?"

"It won't be secret there."

"Does it have to be?"

"Yes. It's much better that way. I have a refrigerator and a table in my basement."

"What about your parents?"

"Because you're not Jewish?"

"Not Jewish? I meant because I'm a girl."

Harvey stood up and dusted sugar off himself. "Why should my parents care about that? I can have a girl over. It's not like we're going together, right?"

For a brief second I was hurt; then I realized Harvey was just joking.

"Right," I said.

Part II

· 1 ·

"I'm sorry," said my mother with a slightly nasal voice as if she were addressing a meeting instead of just my father and me at the table, "that there are no vegetables."

"That's okay," I said. I broke the crust on my chicken pot pie and watched yellow sauce run over the prongs of my fork.

"There are *some* vegetables in here," I said. Rapidly in my mind I was debating strategies for getting my parents to give me written permission to work on the dog. Harvey told me Mr. Hanson wanted the permission right away so we could start immediately.

If I waited to ask, supper might get tense, and then someone, most likely my mother, would take it out on me. No matter when I told her about the dog, she might have a fit on general principles. My father, who had tried to get us to go vegetarian last year, might be especially annoyed tonight about the lack of vegetables. His annoyance might make him automatically say no to the project. But if he did that, my mother might get annoyed with him and side with me. Her approval was more important at the moment. He would go along with it later. You see what I mean about the UN? It was tricky.

"I'm going to enter the science fair," I finally said, lifting into the air two peas and a small carrot cube.

My father looked up. "Really!" he said with more enthusiasm than I had anticipated. Nothing annoyed my mother more than my father being too jolly.

"Well, it's not a big deal," I said, playing things down. "I was picked by my science teacher." (That was more or less the truth. Mr. Hanson said they *had* been talking about me before I came in the room.) "The high school show is December sixth, the county show is in January, and the state fair is in March. You can win a hundred dollars locally, three hundred dollars for county, and a thousand dollars for state."

My mother asked for the salt and said, "Well, the money would be nice, but if I were you, I wouldn't get my hopes set on winning. There's a lot of competition involved with these shows. Some parents even do the projects for their kids. I trust you don't expect that from us, but you should know what you're up against."

"I know," I said, wondering why my mother was always so negative. It seemed no matter what I did, she disapproved.

"When I was in high school, I entered the science fair, remember, Heather?" said my father. "I made a machine that used a can of Sterno for energy, and when I lit the Sterno, all the paint on the machine burned. Whew! What a stench!"

My mother put pie to her mouth. Her expressionless eyes were on my father.

"Mr. Hanson has an idea he thinks will win," I said, knowing I had to get this part over with and dreading it. "It's to put together a skeleton of a dog. Mr. Hanson found a dead dog this morning on the side of the road. He says that no one owned it, that he will help us, and that 3-D entries are usually the best."

My parents put down their forks and stared at me.

"I know it sounds weird," I continued. "But kids have done cats and won. Mr. Hanson said so."

"I'll say it sounds weird," said my mother, shaking her head. "I can hardly eat." Nevertheless, she went back to her pie and slowly continued to eat it.

"You say the dog is already dead?" asked my father.

"Yes."

"And this was your teacher's idea?"

"Yes."

"And he's going to help you?"

"Yes."

"Lisa said all that before," said my mother with a sigh.

"And you say it's been done before with cats?" asked my father, ignoring her to pursue his line of inquiry.

I couldn't tell what they were getting at. I imagine they didn't know either. "Don't you think," I said, quoting Harvey and trying to sound earnest, the way grown-ups like, "that it would be better for the dog to be used for an educational project than to be buried in the ground with worms?"

They both stopped chewing.

"I need a letter tomorrow from you to say I can do it," I explained. "It was an honor to be picked. It would be a shame if Mr. Hanson had to get someone else."

They started chewing again. Then my father swallowed and shook his head. " 'Dear Mr. Biology Teacher,' " he said. " 'My daughter has permission to cut up a dead dog and put it back together again. Sincerely, Bill Barnes.' You mean like that?" He laughed.

"Sure," I said.

" 'Dissect' would sound better," said my mother, "and 'reassemble its skeleton.' "

"Yes, that's much better," I added quickly.

My father looked at me. "Your mother and I are very proud of you," he said. I knew he didn't mean it. I mean, he may have meant it, but that's not why he said it. He said it because it was what fathers in happy families say, and he still wanted to believe we were a happy family. As for me, I was relieved to have permission but slightly queasy inside because there had never been a chance for me to say whom I was doing the project with and where we were doing it.

One thing at a time, I decided.

· 2 ·

"You can make a poem look like anything," said Ms. Turner. With a long thin arm she wrote letters all over the board.

TO THE GROUND
a n d   d i e

"Who can read it?" she asked.

Marty Bagdesarian's hand shot up in the air. He was the smartest boy in class.

"Marty?"

" 'Autumn leaves fall to the ground and die.' May I ask a question?"

"Of course."

"How is that a poem?"

Ms. Turner set the chalk in the tray. "Well,

of course, it's not *really* a poem. I just wrote it to show you that the way words *look* sometimes affects the meaning of a poem. Now —"

"In what way —"

"We'll discuss it more later, Marty. For now I'd like each of you to think of a word, a phrase, or a sentence and write it in a way that looks its meaning. Come on, no talking, just open your notebooks to a blank page and write. Don't be afraid to be creative. Let your imaginations soar."

Everyone was grumbling.

"It's fun!" insisted Ms. Turner. "Look!" She pointed to her poem on the board. "Look at all the punctuation rules you can break!"

"Can you break spelling rules?" asked Marty.

"Well, no."

"What if they contribute to the meaning of the poem?"

"Quiet, Bagdesarian, I can't think," someone said.

Ms. Turner looked grateful and sat down at her desk.

In my notebook I wrote.

Dear Denise,
I can't come over this afternoon to see your new skirt because I'm working on a science fair project. Now don't make fun! I'll tell you about it later. I *know* Harvey was sitting next to Ellen Goldberg again at lunch, but yesterday in gym she told me she doesn't like him, and besides, he asked *me* to

work on the science fair project with him, not her. They're just friends, that's all.

Lisa

"How is everyone doing?" Ms. Turner rose from her desk. Quickly I turned the page and wrote down a poem I thought she would like. She walked up and down the aisle enthusiastically. "I'm seeing some very interesting work," she said. "All right now. Who would like to come up and write your poem on the board?"

No hands went up.

"Lisa?"

I groaned. It was awful being a good student, not a good student like Marty, but a good, *nice* student. Teachers exploit you. "Can't I just read it aloud?" I asked.

"But that's not the point, is it?" said Ms. Turner.

I dragged myself to the board. I hate to get up in front of the class. Wishing I had written a better poem, I wrote:

NIGHTTIME NIGHTTIME NIGHTTIME
NIGHTTIME NIGHTTIME NIGHTTIME
NIGHTTIME NIGHTTIME NIGHTTIME
NIGHTTIME NIGHTTIME NIGHTTIME
q u i e t

It took me forever. As soon as I finished the last *t*, I put the chalk down and retreated to my seat.

"That's lovely," said Ms. Turner. "Who will read it?"

" 'Nighttime, nighttime, nighttime, night-time, nighttime, nighttime, nighttime, night-time, nighttime, nighttime, nighttime, night-time, quiet.' " said Marty. "May I ask how *that* is a poem?"

"It's a poem," said someone, "because you can feel dark, heavy night coming down and everything else is quiet."

"Yes," said Ms. Turner, ignoring Marty. "Is that what you meant to communicate, Lisa?"

I tried not to think of the moment in the bulldozer when Harvey had put his hand on the back of my head. All the kids were look-ing at me and I was afraid they could see into my mind. "I was thinking of a forest," I said.

Someone suggested I could have made trees in the poem, and someone else went to the board to show how she had made a poem that looked like a tree. Marty Bagdesarian never got his question answered, and I went back to dreaming about Harvey Burns. After school we were going to his house for the first time.

· 3 ·

Mr. Hanson's car was a little red Fiesta. Harvey sat in the back with the dog in a plastic bag set in a carton on his lap, and I sat in the front, holding a box of bottles of formaldehyde, stainless steel trays, scalpels, and tweezers. The black shelf under Mr. Hanson's glove compartment contained old maps, a Reese's peanut butter cup wrapper, and a green chiffon scarf. I looked over at Mr. Hanson. From the side you could see he had combed his hair forward to hide a bald spot.

"So both your parents went along with this," he said. "Great."

"Mine want me to be a doctor," said Harvey.

"You'd make a good one," said Mr. Hanson, inserting the key into the ignition. His key chain said NO NUKES. "I used to think I'd be a doctor too."

"What happened?"

"Oh, I don't know. When I came back from Vietnam, it seemed like the easiest thing to do was become a teacher." Mr. Hanson started the engine, then he cut it. "Oh, I forgot I have something for you." He reached into the inside breast pocket of his jacket and took out a black and white photo of me and Harvey dancing. Harvey had his lips closed and his head up high. My hair was shiny on top, and I couldn't see any of the cut-off parts.

"Thank you," I said, a little self-conscious about how close we were dancing.

"Good depth of field," said Harvey. He didn't seem embarrassed at all. "What kind of a camera were you using?"

"Nikon F3," said Mr. Hanson, starting the car again. "My kitchen is set up so I can turn it into a darkroom."

Harvey tapped me lightly, once, on the

shoulder with the photo. I put it in my sketch-book. I couldn't wait to show it to Clearlight and Denise. All across town Harvey and Mr. Hanson talked about cameras.

"Turn left," said Harvey. "It's that white house on the right, the one with the hedge."

Harvey's house looked like an embassy. The lawn didn't have a blade of crabgrass in it. The front door was red. Just as we approached it, it opened. A woman with golden hair and a powder blue sweater and slacks set greeted us.

"Come in, everyone," she said warmly. Her pink earrings were shaped like scallop shells.

I stepped forward quickly and sank into something so soft I gasped and had to look down. The carpeting was about two inches thick. It was blueish gray and went every-where, through all the doorways and up the stairs.

"Say, Lisa, if you'll just move on ahead, Harvey can get in with the dog," said Mr. Hanson.

I jumped aside and bumped into a small white table on top of which was a round green vase holding white chrysanthemums. I felt clumsy about the table and sad about the flowers because my mother used to put flowers around our house too. She didn't do it anymore. We paraded through the dining room; this time I was last. The table was made of thick glass and made me wonder if the Burnses could see everyone's laps when they ate.

The kitchen was white with brown clay tiles on the floor. The counter was real wood, and on it was a square blue platter piled high with brownies. We went down into the basement through a door just past the brownies.

"We haven't fixed up the basement yet," apologized Mrs. Burns. "If we had, I don't know if I would like the idea of a dead dog down here, even though it *is* educational."

"I always try to see that kids of Harvey and Lisa's caliber are challenged," said Mr. Hanson.

"I'm glad to hear you say that," said Mrs. Burns, "because, as I'm sure you realize, Horace Mann is a very fine school. Harvey went there last year, you know."

"I don't mind saying we have an excellent science department right here in Bar Ferry," said Mr. Hanson proudly. "Now then, Harvey, this is just perfect. You can set up the dissection trays right here on the table: one for the dog, one for throwaways, and one for the bones. Each time you take the dog from the plastic bag, seal the bag, and put it back in the refrigerator. When you're done for the day, put the dog back in the bag and close it tightly, making sure all surfaces are covered with formaldehyde. Do you have ventilation down here?"

"Why, yes," said Mrs. Burns, smiling. "There's an old fan over there, and we have more if you need them. My husband and I are in the contemporary fan business."

"Is that so?" asked Mr. Hanson.

"We have a company called Fan-tastic, Inc. We just opened a small factory here in the old train station. That's why we moved here."

"That's very interesting," said Mr. Hanson, visibly impressed. "I might like to take my students on a field trip to visit you someday."

"You'd be most welcome," said Mrs. Burns.

I saw Harvey roll his eyes and tap his feet impatiently. Mr. Hanson turned to me. "Well, what do you say, kids? Going to start today? Might as well."

"How about a little snack first?" said Mrs. Burns. "Lisa and Harvey might be hungry."

Lisa and Harvey. I loved the accepting way she said that. Her voice was low and velvety, the kind that tells fairy tales to children.

· 4 ·

We sat at the dining room table, and right away I noticed you *could* see everyone's lap. I wished my boots were polished. Mrs. Burns kept asking me if I wanted more, so I wound up taking thirds. So did Harvey. Mr. Hanson patted his stomach and said he'd like to but really couldn't.

Mrs. Burns and Mr. Hanson got talking about bugs and trees. "Do you think we should spray?" she asked.

"No, I don't," said Mr. Hanson firmly. "The poison harms all the insects, the good ones and the bad, not to mention the birds that eat them. Best to let Nature run her course."

Looking unconvinced, Mrs. Burns turned to me and asked how I would get home each day.

"Bus seven," I said too fast, almost choking on my food. "It goes right by my street."

"Fine, dear," she said, looking away as if she knew I couldn't bear to have her watch me cough.

"Let's get going," said Harvey, pushing back his chair.

Downstairs he took out the dog and opened the plastic bag on the table. The formaldehyde stank.

"Whew!" I said, but I was really happy because finally we were alone.

"I'll turn on the fan," he said. "Who's going to make the first cut?"

The dog was all stiff and wet.

"I wonder if it was some kid's," I said.

"It didn't have a tag."

I pointed to an ear. "Look how chewed up the poor thing is."

"It was just a stupid mutt," said Harvey. "You go first."

"Why me?"

"It's my house. You want me to do everything?"

"You're just squeamish," I teased.

"I am not."

But when I looked at Harvey, I saw he really was. At that moment I had a funny feeling I knew Harvey better than he knew himself.

"Scalpel," I said, putting out my hand. With one swift slash I cut the belly of a dog just as Mr. Hanson had told me. I went right through to the interior cavity and was amazed to recognize so many of the organs. "Look," I shouted. "There's the stomach, the small intestines, the spleen, and the liver!"

Harvey bolted up the stairs.

When he came down, he was carrying a small white plastic garbage can. "I thought we might need this for scraps," he said.

I had already put the organs in the tray.

"We're not doing a project on them," said Harvey. "Just throw them away."

"Not until I sketch them," I said. I went over and washed my hands in the basement sink. With my back to him I said, "For someone who dissected a fetal pig, you sure are squeamish, Harvey Burns."

"I never said I *did* a pig. I said I was *going* to do a pig for extra credit if I stayed at Mann."

That wasn't what I remembered, but I didn't say anything. I sat on a stool with my sketch pad, took out the photo, and looked at it. His mother had said our names together as if she had expected they would always be that way, and now there was a photo to prove how we could dance.

Out of the corner of my eyes I watched Harvey gingerly pull out more entrails. He had put on plastic gloves.

I put the photo away and began to sketch. The liver was so soft and dense I soon became absorbed trying different ways to render its surface. Harvey and I worked quietly, busily, intensely, like doctors during an operation, and I thought: We could do that. We could become a famous medical team. Dr. Burns and Dr. Barnes. No, maybe I wouldn't do it the women's lib way. "Dr. Burns and Dr. Burns, could you come here right away? We have a rare emergency only you two can handle."

The famous husband-wife medical team, Dr. Burns and Dr. Burns today completed the first heart/lung/kidney transplant in medical history.

Hello, is Dr. Burns there? Which one did you want? It doesn't matter. I hear you're both fabulous. Well, thank you very much. What can I do for you?

Harvey dropped the dog back into the bag and said, "Well, that's that."

"Do you want to see?" I held up my sketch.

"That's pretty good," he said.

I turned the page and showed him another sketch.

"Not too bad," he said hesitantly, as if, for some reason, he didn't want to compliment me too much. He peeled off one of his bloody gloves and dropped it in the garbage can. "That was good, by the way, the way you were acting upstairs."

"What do you mean?"

"You know, like a brain."

"Like a brain?"

"Yeah, I told my mother you were real smart, and I was glad she could see it today. That was good, the way you were listening so intently to Mr. Hanson when he was talking about spraying."

"But I wasn't . . ."

"What I'm trying to say, Lisa, is that I think it's best if you keep on acting that way. I mean, I hate to tell you this, but, well, I've decided I like Ellen Goldberg. My mom knows that too." As he said that, his chin was tipped up, and he was looking right down his nose at me.

"Oh," I said as if he had told me the weather. I shut my pad, put it in my book bag, and walked up the cellar stairs. I didn't say bye, and Harvey didn't follow. His mother wasn't in the kitchen, or in the dining room, or in the front hall. I closed the front door behind me and headed straight for the bus stop.

You might think I'd be crying by this time, but I wasn't, and I'll tell you why. Something about Harvey had bugged me. I liked him, but I couldn't completely trust him. He was too unpredictable, and it wasn't worth it. It was better not to have a boyfriend than a boyfriend like him. He was too conceited.

At first I swore I would never speak to Harvey Burns again for my whole life. But then on the bus I changed my mind. I *would* speak to him but only about the dog project. I would stick with the dog project just to show him that his rudeness didn't mean a thing to me. When I became a famous doctor, if someone ever asked me about Harvey Burns, I wouldn't even remember who he was.

What if he were wheeled into the emergency room and I had to operate on him. He'd say, "Lisa, remember me? Remember our dog?" And I'd say, "Dr. Barnes to you. What dog?"

· 5 ·

"Lisa May Barnes, you really are something, cutting up a dog like that," said Mrs. Hall. I had stopped at the Halls' on my way home, I guess to try out my new attitude toward Harvey. "And what about you, Denise Hamilton Hall, what are you cutting up for the science fair?"

Denise made a face and skimmed a miniature marshmallow off the surface of her cocoa. She popped it into her mouth. "I'm not doing anything for the science fair, Mother, and you know perfectly well that I'm not."

To an outsider that might have sounded fresh, but that was the way the Halls talked. Mrs. Hall wasn't upset. She went on to say that since Sergio Valente had made such a fortune with his designer jeans, maybe Denise should go into sportswear fashion too.

But Denise was more interested in me. "You really don't like him anymore?" she asked.

"No," I said. "I decided today. He's too stuck on himself, and besides that, he's squeamish. He couldn't even cut up the dog. I had to do it all myself."

They both made a face and said they couldn't either.

"But the point is he said he *wanted* to," I complained. "He talked me into it. Anyway, I'm going along with the project because we'll probably win. That would be good for getting into college. I may become a doctor."

Denise and her mother looked at each other.

"You won't tell anyone about the dog, will you?" I asked. "It's supposed to be a secret."

They shook their heads solemnly.

"I like Tommy," I announced.

"And I like Bobby!" said Denise. "We can double-date!"

"That's a good idea," I said.

Mrs. Hall seemed proud as a mother hen. "You girls are going to have a marvelous year. I can just tell." She raised her eyebrows at me. "And quite frankly, Lisa, I think you have made a very wise choice."

"What do you mean?" I asked, annoyed at the way her eyebrows were raised.

"Oh, well, you know, dear, it's always better to stick with people of your own faith. Not that it makes any difference, of course, at your age, but still, there's no point —"

"My own faith? I don't go to church."

"No, but still, well, weren't you baptized?"

"No."

"I see." Mrs. Hall squinted and pursed

her lips. She seemed to be thinking. "Of course, it's not really just a matter of faith," she finally said. "Jewish people usually prefer their young folk to date each other. At least that's the way it was when I grew up. If a Jewish boy went out with a non-Jewish girl, his parents had a fit! They would threaten to disown him."

"That's not the way it is today," I said.

"No, I suppose not. Still, Jews like to stick together. They're instinctively tribal. Maybe they do better in business that way."

I pushed my cup away from me and cleared my throat. "Mrs. Hall," I said firmly, but then I couldn't go on. I was going to say, "What you just said was prejudiced. If Harvey heard you, he would have been furious." But I didn't say it, because at that moment I didn't feel like being on Harvey's side of anything.

Denise piped up to fill the gap I had left in the conversation. "Well, I'm glad, Lisa, that you don't like Harvey anymore because I'm pretty sure he likes Ellen Goldberg. Haven't you noticed how he's always flirting with her?"

"Goldberg?" Mrs. Hall sang out. "I hate to say I told you so." She put the milk in the refrigerator, shut the door, and leaned back against it. The Halls' refrigerator was brown and always layered with notes, clippings, and coupons. Mrs. Hall smiled at me with pity, and I felt like throwing the bag of marshmallows at her. I was getting as touchy as Harvey.

On my way home I wondered if now might be the right time to tell my parents I was doing the project with Harvey. "You have nothing to worry about," I could say in case they asked about going to his house. "Not with a boy like Harvey Burns. He only likes Jewish girls." But I wasn't sure if my mother would believe me. I decided to wait until after she actually had seen me go out with Tommy.

As for the photo Mr. Hanson gave me, I was going to rip it up, but I just couldn't. I finally decided to put it under my slips. When I got older, I'd probably want to look at it for laughs.

Inside me, I have to admit, something did hurt. But I told myself it was like a paper cut that hurts your finger and keeps throbbing even though you know it isn't serious and will go away in a few days. "A paper cut on the heart," I said to myself. I liked that phrase. I even wrote it down.

NOTHING
hurts
hurts
hurts
hurts
hurts
like a paper cut on the heart.

I think even Marty Bagdesarian would have agreed that was a poem.

The next day at school I ignored Harvey completely. At lunch Denise got up her nerve and asked Bobby and Tommy to sit with us, and they did.

"So what's with this science project you and Burns are doing?" Tommy asked gruffly.

I looked at Denise.

"I didn't say what it *was*," she said.

"Mr. Hanson picked us to do it. It's a good idea except for the part where I have to go to Harvey's house after school to work on it." I groaned.

"You don't like that?" asked Tommy as he bit into a hot dog.

"It's gross," I said.

"Lisa says he's conceited and squeamish," said Denise. "Anybody want my coleslaw? I can't bear cabbage."

"He quit football just because someone called him a kike," said Bobby.

I put a potato chip into my mouth and chomped on it noisily as if I couldn't care less about anything.

"Nobody meant it," said Tommy. "Everybody gets called names like that. They call me Tommy the Wop and call Bobby Mick-Dick."

Bobby blushed.

"Burns is just your normal weirdo," said Tommy. "It's best to leave a guy like that alone."

"Yeah," I agreed, but then I added, "I figure it's worth it, though, to work with him on the science fair."

Everybody looked at me skeptically.

After school Harvey got on the bus first and sat way in the back on the seat that goes across the whole bus. I sat forward near the driver. When the bus stopped at his stop, he got out the back door and walked ahead of me to his house. I didn't bother to catch up. He left the front door open, and when I walked in, he was hanging up his jacket.

"Where's your mother?" I asked.

"At the train station," he said. He didn't offer to take my jacket, so I left it on. "But don't worry," he said sarcastically, "she'll be back."

"I'm not worried," I said. He was so rude!

As we entered the kitchen, I noticed the same blue platter on the counter, this time piled high with blond brownies, the kind with chocolate chips inside. Nearby were two dark blue plastic mugs, two clean red dessert plates, and a black napkin holder filled with big white paper napkins, the large, thick kind my mother buys for holidays.

Propped up against a white roasting pan was a small square piece of blue graph paper with the name "sara burns" in red letters at the top, all lower case. The note said, "hello to lisa. milk in the fridge. put roast beef in oven, set for one hour defrost and one hour cooking. 325°."

Harvey took a package out of the freezer, unwrapped it, and set it in the white pan. He punched some numbers on the stove and stuck the pan in the oven.

"Is that a microwave?" I asked.

"Yeah," he said.

"I thought they gave out radiation," I said.

Harvey shrugged and took another brownie. He poured himself some milk and set the carton on the counter.

I looked out the window at a kidney-shaped swimming pool covered with gray-green vinyl for the winter. Then I poured myself some milk. Harvey put his cup and plate in the dishwasher and went downstairs. I finished my milk, put my cup and plate in the dishwasher too, and followed him, my Frye boots making a loud, awkward clatter on his wooden cellar steps.

Harvey turned on the lights, and I put down my books. He turned on the radio, and I pulled out my sketchbook. He went over to the refrigerator, and I sat on the stool. Mr. Hanson was ordering a book on dog anatomy, which would help me, but for now he said to erase all shadings.

"If you shade the liver in, Lisa," he had said, "you make it look as if you knew what it is made of. Do little dots instead. That way you indicate that it's made up of something smaller, like fibers or cells."

I erased a shaded area completely and dotted it. Harvey came over and looked critically at the sketch. "What did you do that for?" he asked.

"Mr. Hanson told me to," I said.

Harvey took out the dog and worked tensely. After a while he threw a leg into a pan. "You can do the other one," he said.

I held the paw in my left hand and the scalpel in my right. I slit the skin and pulled it off. It was attached to the dog by filmy white tissue that tore away easily from the muscles underneath.

"How do you feel?" asked Harvey.

"I told you yesterday I don't mind," I said. And I didn't, especially now that the fur of the dog was gone. The muscles were smooth and fairly distinct. I stopped to sketch them.

"It will take forever if you always stop," said Harvey.

"Not really," I said. "You do one side fast, and I'll do one slow. We have to have the sketches. Mr. Hanson said so."

Harvey cut sloppily and threw chunks of flesh into the scrap tray.

You could *never* be a doctor, I thought.

Neither his mother nor his father came home the entire afternoon. In a way I was insulted that they trusted me so much. "She's such a brain we don't have to worry about her," I could imagine them saying. In spite of my annoyance, I worked steadily and sometimes became so absorbed I didn't even listen to the radio. In a way I was a brain, and in a way I was glad.

Walking to the bus stop, I thought how much better it was now that nothing was going on between me and Harvey. "Everything's an opportunity," Clearlight always said, and she was right. Getting involved

with Harvey, even though he was a total
jerk, had given me the opportunity to realize
I wanted to be a doctor. I couldn't help thinking about the muscles and tissue in my legs
and wondering what it was that makes bodies
work and stay alive.

<h2 style="text-align:center">· 7 ·</h2>

The next day Mrs. Burns was home. She
smiled at me as if she really liked me, and I
wondered if she knew I wasn't Jewish. She
asked how the project was going.

"You want to see how far we got?"

"No, no, thank you, dear," she said. "Every
night Harvey shows his father, and last night
I took a peek too. That was enough for now,
I think. I'm not quite as scientifically minded
as you are, I don't believe."

Downstairs I said, "Let's get all the flesh
off so you can boil the bones this weekend."

"Me? Why do I have to do all the boiling?"
Harvey's petulance annoyed me. He annoyed
me, period. At school he was always holding
hands with Ellen Goldberg in the halls, and
today at lunch I couldn't think of one topic to
talk about with Tommy.

"What do you mean, why?" I asked. "Mr.
Hanson said the bones have to boil first, then
bake several hours. Do you expect me to sit
around here waiting for that? I have better
things to do. You *have* to do it because it's
your house. Maybe your mother will help
you."

"Why don't you take some of the bones home with you?"

"You've got to be kidding."

"Why not? We're supposed to be in this equal."

I pressed my teeth together and felt the sides of my jaw go out. "All right," I said. "If it makes you feel better, I'll take half the dog home with me on the bus."

"Nah, I was only kidding," said Harvey, laughing. "Like I always said, you're too gullible."

I took out my sketchbook and started drawing the dog's pitiful head. Out of the corner of my eyes I could see Harvey still grinning at me like a goon. I drew each wet strand of hair on the mashed-up ear.

Harvey was coming closer, still grinning. I felt ice-cold and began to draw the ear as carefully as I could. As I did, Harvey knelt down in front of me and stared at me grinning, grinning, grinning with those stupid shiny braces. I was furious, but at the same time something inside me was dying to laugh.

"Harvey, really."

"Aha! The lady smiles, and the lights from her sparkling eyes blind the poor knight, who faints on the drawbridge beneath her." With that, Harvey fell flat on his back on the floor right in front of me.

"Really," I said again, trying to sound disgusted. I brushed my hair back and looked around, bored. I glanced down. Harvey had his eyes closed. I pretended he wasn't there and started sketching the ear again. Then I couldn't help it. I started sketching Harvey. His cheekbones were prominent, and his bushy eyebrows almost met in the middle.

He opened his eyes.

"The lady gazes down sorrowfully at the poor knight and swoons at his misfortune."

I turned my page quickly and started a new sketch of the dog's head. Harvey jumped up. "Let me see that other page."

"No."

"Come on," pleaded Harvey.

"No!" I said, holding the pad tightly on my lap.

"What would Mr. Hanson say if he heard you weren't showing me your sketches?" Harvey put his hands on the pad too.

I pulled the pad away from Harvey and held it against my chest. Underneath I could feel my heart pounding. "Stop!" I cried out. "If you don't stop, I'll call your mother! I know she's up there!"

Harvey put up his hands in surrender. "Hey, forget it," he said in a cool voice. "I was just trying to lighten things up, but forget it. If you want this to be strictly business, it'll be strictly business."

He went back to his tray.

I went back to my sketch. Neither of us talked. I almost said I was sorry, but I didn't want to give Harvey another chance to start in on me again. It was embarrassing to work in such a loaded atmosphere, but I managed to make two fairly accurate sketches. After we had finished cleaning up, Harvey put his hand on my arm, and I jumped.

"I just want to tell you, if you don't want to come here anymore, it's okay. I understand. You can do the whole project at your house and take all the credit. I don't blame you for hating me."

I looked into Harvey's eyes and tried to figure out if he was sincere or not. He seemed to be, but I didn't trust him. "Two more days, and we'll be past this stage of the project," I said.

That night I put the sketch of Harvey under my slips with the photo, not because of Harvey, but because it was the best drawing I had ever done.

· 8 ·

The next two days, thank heaven, Harvey's mother was home. Harvey didn't fool around anymore. He didn't act goony or snotty, just normal. But I had no interest in him no matter how he acted. I worked hard on my dissections and sketches almost as if he weren't there, though of course I knew he was. I had begun to feel obsessed about winning first prize because it was the only thing that made going to Harvey's house every afternoon make sense.

By four o'clock that Friday afternoon I was exhausted and satisfied with the pile of bones we had amassed. Harvey and I threw out all the scraps of flesh and took the pan of bones up to show Harvey's mother. She was outside planting daffodil and tulip bulbs.

"Put them in the refrigerator, and we'll boil them tomorrow," she said, grimacing. She put her hand on her back and stood up. "Would you like a ride home, Lisa?"

"Oh, no, thank you," I said.

"I have to get some bulb food," said Mrs. Burns.

"But the bus is so easy," I said, aghast. I didn't want her to see my house. My father had a "new" VW wreck on the front lawn. "For parts," he had said. He had promised my mother to move it in a day, but it was still there.

"Don't be silly," said Mrs. Burns. "You go get in the car, and I'll just get my purse. Do you want to come too, Harvey?"

"Can I drive?" he asked.

"Well," Mrs. Burns looked around as if she expected to consult someone. "I guess so."

I couldn't move. It was after five thirty. My mother might be home. I hadn't told her about going to Harvey's house. Plus I didn't want her to meet Mrs. Burns, or Mrs. Barnes to meet her. "I — I — I can't . . ." I stammered.

Harvey looked at me strangely, "Maybe she should take the bus," he said to his mother, as if he somehow knew what I was worried about.

Mrs. Burns laughed. "What's the matter with you two? Hurry up and get in."

Harvey and Mrs. Burns got in the front seat. Numbly I got in the back. The inside of their car was black and clean. As we drove down out of the hilly section of town where the Burnses lived, through the old two-family section of town, and into the flat section where I lived, I prayed that my mother would not be home.

Mrs. Burns turned her head around to me. "I suppose a girl like you knows all about why trees change."

I couldn't reply.

Harvey turned on the radio.

"Rivergate," said Mrs. Burns. "What an interesting name."

Too late I thought to have them drop me off at the corner or at Denise's. Why wasn't my brain working? Because I was half-dead.

"Which way?" asked Harvey.

He was pretending he didn't know. "Turn left," I said. "Now right. Now left."

We went down my street, and there was the VW on the lawn, and there was my mother getting out of her old red Volkswagen in the driveway with a bag of groceries.

I wanted to fall through the floor and be a speck of dirt on the road that people would drive over all year long.

· 9 ·

Before Harvey completely stopped, I jumped out and said, "Bye, thanks," hoping he would take off like the Dukes of Hazzard. I think he would have too, but for the fact that his mother opened her door. She was walking around the car toward my mother. My mother stopped and stared. Her stocking had a run. She didn't return Mrs. Burns's smile.

"Mom," I said in a rush, "meet Mrs. Burns. She's just dropping me off. Well, I have so much homework I'd better go in and do it."

"Sara Burns," said Mrs. Burns in her deep, calm voice, graciously extending her hand.

My mother shifted the groceries so she could shake. "How do you do, Mrs. Burns?" she said with a sudden, horrid smile. She looked toward the car. "And I suppose you're ..."

"Harvey," said Harvey, and as he said it, his voice squeaked the way a lot of boys' voices do, but I'd never heard his do it before.

"I'll take the bag in," I said, hurrying with it toward the house.

"Isn't it fascinating what the two of them are doing?" asked Mrs. Burns.

"Lisa?" asked my mother.

I looked around at her and pleaded with my eyes that she wouldn't make a scene.

"Oh, yes," my mother said, slightly shrill. "What the two of them are doing ... it's just wonderful! I can't tell you how thrilled I am!"

Mrs. Burns glanced over at me, and I think she knew that I wished my mother had a lower voice, new stockings, and a house that didn't look like the one three doors down. "We'll see you Monday, Lisa," she said.

"Monday?" shrieked my mother. Her voice made me wince. I couldn't stand it any longer, so I ran inside. I slammed the groceries on the kitchen counter and hurried up to my room.

· 10 ·

"Lisa Barnes, you get down here!"

I lay on my bed and didn't move.

"I said get down here!" She was calling from the bottom of the stairs. I still didn't move.

"Lisa Barnes, if you don't get down here . . ." I heard her angry footsteps coming up the stairs, so I ran out of my room at the top. She stood below me, glaring up and gripping the banister.

"How dare you humiliate me like that?"

I look down at her. Her face was all worked up and ugly. I didn't know what to say. I thought of Mrs. Burns driving away and hoped she was saying to Harvey something like: "Lisa's not very much like her mother, is she?"

"I asked *How dare you?*"

How can you answer a question like that? Really? It doesn't make any sense. I didn't *dare* do anything. Things just happened.

Suddenly my mother brought her hand up and smacked it flat against the wall. *"Lisa!"* she shrieked. "Talk to me!" Then she crumpled up on the stairs. All I could do, it seemed, was stare down at her speechlessly. I felt huge.

"You don't need me anymore," she said in a tight, low voice. "Neither does your father. His dreams are separate from mine. I can't help him design solar homes. Half the time I don't know what he's talking about. And you. You have Mrs. Hall and now Mrs. Burns. I saw how you were looking at her. You were ashamed of me."

I crouched down on the top step and pressed my chest against my knees. I wanted to say, "But I do need you, Mom. So does Dad." And I was going to say it, I really was. I was just trying to get up the nerve. It was so difficult to begin.

"Mom, I . . ."

"Those people, are they Jewish?" she suddenly asked. "Are they the ones redoing the train station? I suppose they're *very* interesting to you."

"Mom, it's nothing," I said. "Don't worry. Look. I'll tell you everything. Last Friday night Harvey Burns walked me home from the dance. You're right. He *is* Jewish. But he doesn't like *me*. The fact is he only likes Jewish girls. He likes Ellen Goldberg. But in school Mr. Hanson picked him and me to do the science fair project together, so we've become . . . friends. That's all, really. *Really*."

My mother looked at me suspiciously, and I wondered if what I had said was true. Did Harvey like only Jewish girls? Had he and I become friends?

"Why didn't you tell me you were doing the science fair project with him?" asked my mother.

"I didn't think you'd understand. See, the thing is we're working on the dog at his house after school because we're trying to keep the project secret. I didn't think you'd let me go there."

"You've been going to *his* house?" My mother shook her head in disbelief. I could tell she was starting to get furious again.

"I thought you might say I couldn't go there, and then what would I do? I really want to win, Mom. We have a much better chance if it's a secret!"

Was that also true? Did I really want to win?

My mother sat forward stiffly. Then she let her breath out and collapsed her shoulders. "I see," she said. She put her hand to her mouth and pressed the back of her fist against her lips. No matter how upset I was with my mother, seeing her cry made me feel terrible.

"Do I embarrass you?" she asked.

"No," I whispered, lying.

"Are you telling me the truth?" she asked.

"Yes," I whispered.

She shook her head back and forth, then shuddered and sat still.

"Mom?" I asked quietly after a few moments had passed. "Is it still all right for me to do the project?"

"Oh, God, Lisa," she said. She stood up and walked down the stairs. "I really don't care," she said, shaking her head. "I really don't care."

So that was it. I could do the project with Harvey at Harvey's house because my mother really didn't care. I went back into my room and lay down. I guess I had won some sort of victory, but I felt as if I had lost.

· 11 ·

"Lisa! Telephone!"

Huh? I awoke in confusion. It was still light out. Why had I been sleeping? My father was calling me. Telephone? I jumped up.

"Hello?"

"It's Tommy."

"Tommy."

"You sound funny."

"I just woke up."

"Do you want to go to dinner at the new Dino's at the mall? Mrs. Hall is driving us. You, me, Denise, and Bobby."

"I don't know if I can. Let me ask."

My mother said she didn't really care. "I guess so," I told Tommy.

"Bobby said Denise said to tell you we would pick you up at seven thirty." Tommy sounded like an old pro at dating, which surprised me.

"Okay," I said.

While Mrs. Hall did her Christmas shopping ("I get it all done before Thanksgiving," she had told us in the car, holding up a huge list for all of us to see), the four of us ate at Dino's Italian Eateria and talked about things that had been ruined. Tommy said the World Series had been ruined by too many play-offs and too much rain. Denise said

Puppy Palace, a pet store at the mall that sold only dogs, had been ruined by a new manager who wouldn't let kids hang out there anymore.

"Dino's has *definitely* been ruined," I said, nodding at the new mirrored walls and ferns surrounding us.

"I think it's pretty," said Denise.

"These are the kind of plastic tables they have at McDonald's," I said. "Look underneath. See? No legs. The tables hang out from the wall so the floors can be mopped easily. You want everywhere to look like McDonald's?"

"All McDonald's are different inside," said Denise. "And anyway, I like Dino's. I don't think it's been ruined at all."

"I'll tell you what's been ruined," said Bobby. "Christmas. Christmas shopping in October, it's ridiculous. Christmas is totally commercial."

Denise had a fit. "I don't know how you can say that!" she squealed.

Bobby shrugged.

Tommy rolled a forkful of spaghetti and held it in the air. "It may be commercial, but still, when all is said and done, there is something about Christmas that makes you feel good." He put the spaghetti in his mouth and continued to speak. "But I have to admit, the original meaning has been lost."

"What do you mean?" protested Denise. She was enjoying this conversation, I could tell. "It's Jesus' birthday. Everybody still knows that. You can't escape it. I mean, there's even a creche at the mall. Isn't that amazing when you think about it? People still worship Jesus even though He was born almost two thousand years ago. I think it's excellent."

"Don't tell me you believe Jesus was really the Son of God?" Bobby asked her incredulously.

"Of course I do!" said Denise in a flirty way. "Don't you?"

Bobby, looking macho and wise beyond his years, shook his head. "No way."

"What about you, Tommy?" asked Denise enthusiastically, as if she were running a talk show.

Tommy shrugged. "In a way." We all knew that Tommy's whole family went to eight o'clock mass every Sunday, so his answer was no surprise.

"See, Bobby?" said Denise, nevertheless triumphantly.

"What about Lisa?" Bobby asked.

Everybody looked at me, and I was embarrassed. I looked at Bobby's round freckled face and tried to tell if there was something suspicious there. Was he trying to get me to say something about Harvey's being Jewish? I put down my fork.

"What are you looking at me for?" I asked to give myself time.

"Do you believe Jesus was really the Son of God?" asked Denise impatiently. "You heard us all say what we think."

"I believe in spaghetti," I said.

"What?" said Denise, aghast.

I rolled some pasta on my fork. "Well, spaghetti is made of wheat, right?"

Denise groaned.

"Well, right?"

"Right," said Tommy.

"Okay. We eat the wheat. That wheat becomes us. We die and return to the earth. The earth grows new wheat. There is an endless cycle of life and death. All living things are one. That's why I believe in spaghetti." I smiled and put the spaghetti in my mouth. That was a pretty good answer, I thought.

"I don't know about that," said Tommy.

"You think too much, Lisa," said Bobby. "It's not necessary."

"You didn't answer the question," complained Denise.

"I did too," I said, trying not to laugh. Harvey would have thought her question was pretty narrow-minded. He would have liked my reply.

In the car going home Tommy intertwined his fingers with mine, and all I could think of were the small bones Harvey and I had taken out of the dog's paws. I wished I could stop thinking about Harvey, but everything I did seemed to remind me of him. Often it seemed that my thoughts were phrased as messages for him to hear. It was a struggle to accept that Tommy was my boyfriend and that Harvey was a boy who was just my

friend. I wondered how and when we'd start
acting friendly. That was something I looked
forward to.

· 12 ·

The rest of the weekend my mother hardly
talked to anyone. My father spent most of
the time in the basement, and I spent most
of the time on my bed, sometimes reading,
sometimes drawing, sometimes just lying
there and thinking.

I couldn't stand to talk to my parents,
especially my mother. It was as if she and I
were in a neutral zone. She didn't care about
me, and I didn't care about her. Actually I
did care about her unhappiness, but if she
didn't care about mine, there wasn't much
I could do except try not to think about hers.

Monday morning I dragged myself off, late
as usual, to school and went through my
classes like a zombie. At lunch I couldn't
think of a thing to say to Tommy. Denise
asked me if I had cramps, and I said sort of.

When school was over, I got on the bus
before Harvey and sat in my usual seat up
front. I read the sign opposite me about false
teeth cleaning powder. When you think about
it, it's awful; the minute you're born, you
start to die. Parts of your body, like your
teeth, haven't even begun to grow, yet decay
is their certain fate.

The bus driver gunned the engine, and I
wondered if Harvey was going to make it.
At the last minute he climbed on. He walked

past me without a nod, as usual; then something seemed to change his mind. Instead of walking to the back of the bus, he turned and, holding onto one of the straps, read the sign above me as if he didn't know I was there.

I opened my book and laid it on my book bag across my lap. Harvey's knees were right above the pages. The book, a mystery by Rosemary Wells, was good, but I was having a hard time concentrating because the brown corduroy fabric in Harvey's pants was jiggling. He was tapping his foot. I read and reread the same paragraph:

> The plane lurched slightly. A stewardess walking down the aisle did not seem aware of it. She bounced along, smiling frostily. Kathy tensed against her seat and pulled her belt tight. She shut her eyes against the stewardess' inquiring glance. *How like my mother's that smile is,* Kathy thought. *Cold and condensed.*

When the woman next to me got up, Harvey swung down into the vacant spot and acted surprised to see me. Maybe now he was going to start being my friend.

"Hi."

"Hi."

He set his book bag on the floor between his feet and spread his hands out on his thighs. I kept my knees together, but every once in a while his right leg swung over and touched mine. I tried to go back to my reading.

Then someone on the other side of Harvey got up and was replaced by a fat man, so Harvey had to move even closer to me. We were touching shoulder to boot.

On my book bag was a ball-point heart that said LISA AND TOMMY. Denise had drawn it in home ec. I covered it with my book and tried the paragraph for the third time. I had a feeling Harvey was reading over my shoulder. Then he stopped, stretched his leg forward, and reached for something in his pants pocket. It was a small wooden fish.

"I carved it," he said.

I nodded.

"One summer at Camp Mohekah."

"It's very nice," I said.

"Yeah," said Harvey. He turned it over in his hand and said, "Now I know what you mean about your mother. She really seems unhappy."

Suddenly it was as if a balloon had blown up in my chest, blown up so fast the pressure went to my throat and my head. The type on my page blurred. I was starting to cry. I pressed my hand on my eyes. It was stupid; it was ridiculous, but I couldn't stop crying. My shoulders were shaking. "Oh, God," I said, aghast because I said the words out loud, sobbing. I leaned forward and brought my book up to hide my face. As I did, Harvey put his arm around my back. The bus slowed, and he helped me up. Somehow we walked to the door and stepped down. The bus pulled away and left us in a foul-smelling cloud of exhaust.

"Look," said Harvey, fanning the air. "We got off at South Main."

I wiped my face and laughed. "I guess we'll have to walk."

Harvey took my book bag and swung it up with his over his shoulder. "Let's go," he said.

The sky was bright, and most of the leaves were curled up brown in the gutter. Our footsteps were slow and steady on the sidewalk. My left hand was near Harvey's right hand, and the fact that there was more between Harvey and me than plain friendship was suddenly as clear to me as the sky and the leaves.

"You know?" said Harvey. "I like winter best because you can see the real shape of the trees underneath."

"I know just what you mean," I said.

He said he also liked winter best because he liked to ski. He told me about Stowe, Vermont. I said I knew where that was because one July my parents and I had taken the chair lift up Mount Mansfield and I had gone down the mountain on the alpine slide. He said he had done that too, and he wanted to know how my parents got down the mountain, on the slide or on the chair. I said on the chair. He said his did too.

It was easy to talk again.

"You know that fish?" he said. "You can

have it." He reached into his pocket and gave it to me.

I took it from his palm and said, "It's beautiful. Thank you."

"When I carved it, I hoped it would bring someone good luck someday. I had that in mind."

I put the fish in my pocket and let my left hand drop back by my side. The fact that Harvey didn't reach out to take it didn't bother me because I knew there was time and that things between us were somehow settled, no matter what.

· 13 ·

That day, the whole time we worked, we talked. It was the first time we were completely relaxed together. We talked about the dog, Mr. Hanson, and music.

"Ellen likes punk," Harvey said, "but I don't. We fight about it all the time."

At first I was upset when he brought up her name, but then I realized that for some reason Harvey wanted to pretend he and I were only friends. But I knew he cared for me more than Ellen. After all, he hadn't given her the fish.

"I know what you mean," I said. "Tommy likes disco, and if there's any music I can't stand, it's disco."

"What kind of music do you like?" asked Harvey.

"Anything, as long as it isn't punk or disco," I said.

"Bach is so squared away," said Harvey.

"Bach, Brahms, and Beethoven. I learned about the three Bs when I took piano lessons."

"They're great," said Harvey. "And you know what I also like? Early rock and roll."

"I love early rock and roll!"

"What's your favorite oldie?" he asked.

" 'In the Still of the Night' by the Five Saints," I said, and I started singing it. Harvey came right in with the shoo-be-doos. I could have hugged him, he was so perfect for me. But I didn't want to seem too pushy.

At the top of the stairs the door opened. "Harvey, I'm just going over to the temple with a pie," Mrs. Burns called down. "Lisa, do you want a ride home?"

"No, thanks, Mrs. Burns."

She didn't insist, and I didn't bother myself with wondering why not and what she thought of my mother. Harvey and I sang "Party Doll," "Poison Ivy," and "Crying in the Chapel" as we worked. We had a great time. Then we cleaned up and went upstairs.

In the hall Harvey spun around with a look of inspiration on his face. "You want to see a model I made when I was nine?"

"No, thanks, I'd better go," I said, because somehow I knew that the model would be upstairs.

"It will only take a minute. Come on. I showed Ellen."

"Well . . ." If Ellen Goldberg had been

upstairs, there didn't seem to be any reason why I couldn't go too.

"We're just friends, right?" Harvey's eyes had a soft twinkle in them.

"Right," I said.

The blue-gray carpet that went up the stairs spread out through the upstairs hall and stopped at Harvey's door. His room had a wooden floor with a red and gray Navajo rug on it. His curtains were red plaid, and his bed had a thick gray comforter on it. I was sure it was real down. On his desk was a white word processor with a screen and a printer.

A wooden bookcase with lift-up glass doors held models of airplanes, spacecraft, ships, tanks, and rifles. The model on the top shelf was a submarine. Harvey took it out. "A lot of parts I had to cut out and sand," he said.

On the wall was a pink and purple water-color of an ocean. In the center was a poem typed on a small piece of paper:

> If someday I should fly,
> If someday I should sail,
> If someday I should ride away,
> I would go where the birds go
> and the salmon in the sea
>
> H.B.

"Don't look at that," said Harvey.
"Did you do it?"

"Yeah, but it's juvenile. Look, here's a model of the first *Apollo* spacecraft."

"It's beautiful."

"Look at this one."

"No, not the model. The poem and the painting. You didn't tell me you did things like that."

"I don't. I mean, not always. I do sometimes. You like that sort of stuff? You want to see more? Here," said Harvey aggressively, taking a sheet of typing paper out of his desk drawer, "take a look at this." Typed on the paper was:

> In New York City was a water bug
> Big and black and round.
> I stepped on it
> And heard it crack.
> Out came its insides
> Yellow like lemon sherbet
> Only warm.
> It kept crawling
> Across the floor.
> That's what I call God.

"I think I like the other one better," I said, trying to be diplomatic.

"What I was trying to say is that if you can keep going with your guts hanging out, that's pretty good."

"True," I said. I paused, then I asked offhandedly. "Did you show this to Ellen?"

"No," said Harvey, putting it back in the drawer. "She wouldn't understand. But if you like it, you can have a copy of the 'Someday' poem. I printed ten copies."

"I write poems too," I said.

· 14 ·

The next day for the first time I got to school early. I waited by my locker until I saw Harvey turn the corner at the end of the hall. "Harvey, look!" I cried, running up to him with my hand on my collar. I had glued a clasp from an old jewelry kit to the back of the fish. "I made the fish into a pin!" I took my hand off my blouse to show him.

Harvey glared at me and the fish as if he had never seen either of us before. He looked shocked and insulted.

"Don't you like it?" I asked.

Harvey glanced around in exasperation. "Lisa," he said, "don't be so obvious. As far as everyone else is concerned, nothing is changed."

"Everyone else? Who are you talking about?"

"Ellen and Tommy. Got it?"

"Yes, I guess so," I said, but not to Harvey. He had turned away and was walking down the corridor.

At first I was confused, but the more I thought about him during my morning classes, the more I realized how seriously Harvey wanted to keep everything between us secret. At lunch he flirted with Ellen Goldberg more than ever, and I showed him I finally understood by flirting nearly as much with Tommy.

I wondered, though, when we would be able to be ourselves again. After school Harvey boarded the bus without saying a word to me and sat in his usual seat in the back. Up front I pretended to read. I had started a new book, *I Am the Cheese* by Robert Cormier. It was about a boy in a mental institution.

When the bus stopped at Harvey's corner, Harvey waited for me, and I understood that now we could relax.

"I like the pin," he said.

"I'm glad," I replied. And that was all we said. We walked side by side the rest of the way silently. Out of the blue I recalled the day when my father and I had walked the Great Gorge in New Hampshire. My mother wasn't with us. The dark path along the gorge had a mysterious quality that made talking seem out of place.

At Harvey's house I reached for the doorknob as if it were my own, then withdrew my hand quickly because it didn't seem right to open his front door. At that very same moment Harvey had reached for the knob too, and for a split second his whole body enveloped mine like a blanket. I was stunned and dizzy, and believe I would have lost my balance altogether if Harvey hadn't caught my arm and helped me through the door. Inside the hall was a man.

"Dad!" said Harvey, letting go of me instantly.

His father looked up at us with consternation on his face. He had gray, frizzy hair that seemed a little too long for his age. His face was thin; he was thin. His tan velour sweat shirt and white painter's pants hung loosely from his hips.

"Dad, um, this is Lisa Barnes," said Harvey, "the really smart girl Mom told you about."

"Hi," I said, putting out my hand like a grown-up.

Mr. Burns shook my hand briefly. "You're the girl who's working on the skeleton with Harvey?" His eyes narrowed, and I could feel him scrutinizing me the way Harvey had done that night from the bleachers. It must be an inherited trait, I thought.

"I'm particularly interested in scientific drawing," I said, folding my arms across my chest.

"Well, it's nice you're assisting Harvey," Mr. Burns said. "I came home to find a fan."

"Want me to help you?" asked Harvey.

We headed toward the basement, passing the plate of cookies left by Mrs. Burns. Mr. Burns went to the part of the cellar opposite where we worked. On his side were stacks of white boxes with FAN-TASTIC, INC. printed on them diagonally in big purple block letters.

"Just go ahead with your work," he said. "Don't mind me."

I got the tray of bones down from the shelf

and picked up the bottle of cement and shook it. "I think the rib pictures are on page sixty-four," I said. "Let's start with that." I could sense that Harvey was extremely nervous, and while I wanted to make him feel better, I had to assert myself a little because I didn't like the idea that I was only "assisting" Harvey.

Harvey opened the book. "First thing," he said in an unusually loud voice, "is to attach the first left rib to the first thoracic vertebra."

I dipped the end of the largest rib in the cement and stuck it to the first vertebra. It held. "I'll sketch it now," I said quite formally.

Harvey cleared his throat. "Let's try another," he said.

Mr. Burns had been moving boxes around, making soft scraping and thumping noises. Now he stopped and seemed to be sawing through cardboard with a knife. I heard him pull something out of a box, put it back in, and come over to our side. He stood next to me, box in hand, as I held the next rib in place. No one spoke.

"Isn't it amazing how well the bones fit?" I finally said.

Mr. Burns made a sound that was half sigh, half laugh. I decided he was being friendly.

"The best parts are the ball and socket joints," I said. Holding up the left femur and the pelvis, I demonstrated how one could fit into the other and rotate.

"When I was in art school," said Mr. Burns thoughtfully, "I did a paper on the relationship of form and function in bones."

I glanced at his hands on the box. His fingertips were red and swollen. He bites his fingernails, I realized. I liked him. He acted a little gruff, but there was something about him I liked.

Harvey put his foot on mine. "Ellen can't stand to see the dog," he blurted out.

I didn't know why Harvey had brought up Ellen Goldberg's name or why he had stepped on my foot.

Mr. Burns made that same funny sigh again. "Well," he said, "it certainly is impressive what you two are doing." Then, lifting the box from the table, he said in a more emphatic tone, "Speaking of design, Harvey, I want you to take a look at the plans I drew for the sukkah." Mr. Burns set the box back down and took from his shirt pocket a folded piece of yellow lined paper, which he passed in front of me to Harvey.

"I'm pretty busy with this project," said Harvey. He stuffed the plans, unopened, in his pants pocket.

"I'd like you to do it," said his father.

Harvey shifted his feet impatiently.

Mr. Burns looked back at the dog and me. "Well, good-bye," he said. "Lisa? Is that your name? It was nice meeting you." He went up the cellar stairs with his fan.

Harvey and I worked in silence for about ten minutes. I knew something was going on, but I wasn't sure what it was. It occurred to me that Harvey suspected his father might be listening to us from the other side of the door. It wasn't until we heard a car leave that Harvey banged his fist on the table.

"That idiot! He drives me up the wall!"

I laughed. "If you think he's bad, you should try having supper with my mother. Compared with her, he's extremely pleasant."

"Extremely pleasant? Do you know what a sukkah is? Look!" Harvey pulled out the yellow paper and opened it. On it was drawn a cute little cabin decorated with fruits and branches.

"What's it for?" I asked.

"It's not *for* anything," said Harvey. "That's just the point. It has to do with some minor Jewish holiday you never heard of. Oh, it's ridiculous. I mean, we just went through Rosh Hashanah and Yom Kippur. For most Jews that's enough, right? But oh, no, not for my father. He's driving me crazy with this Jewish stuff." Harvey looked at me exasperatedly. "Oh, you wouldn't understand," he said in disgust.

"I might," I said. "I know Rosh Hashanah is the Jewish New Year."

"Believe me, Lisa," said Harvey quite adamantly, "you don't understand."

By now I had learned not to push Harvey when he got tense, so I flicked on the radio and went back to work. Harvey worked too, angrily, with lots of sighs and sudden motions. Finally he reached up and turned the radio off.

"What you can't possibly understand," he said, "is that being Jewish is the main thing in my father's life. It didn't use to be, but it is now, and it's driving me crazy. How can knowing that Rosh Hashanah is the Jewish New Year help you understand my father?"

"I suppose it doesn't," I said, continuing to work.

"Well, you're right, it doesn't." Harvey sighed. "Look, two years ago my grandmother died. My father got very depressed. He couldn't work. Then he got religion, and now he's the way he is."

"My mother's depressed too," I said, "but I can't imagine her ever getting religion."

"What started her problem?"

"I don't know," I said. "All I know is she doesn't like me, she doesn't like my father, and she doesn't even much like herself. I guess it's because she worries about money and hates her job."

"Is that all? Come on. I'll show you something."

I followed Harvey up the cellar stairs, and telling myself it was all right because nothing had happened the last time, I followed him up another flight to the upstairs hall and from there into his parents' room. All the colors were pastels except for a huge white comforter on a king-size bed. It was the prettiest, airiest room I had ever been in.

Harvey crossed the carpet to a cream-colored dresser, where he stopped and picked up a small gold frame containing an old, creased photo.

"This was my grandmother," he said. The picture showed a woman trying to smile against the sun. Her hair was wavy and pulled diagonally across her forehead. Her dress was baggy, and she had on ankle strap shoes. She was standing in front of a hedge. She seemed about twenty. On each side of her were young men in white shirts, dark pleated pants, and suspenders.

"Those were her brothers," said Harvey huskily. He pointed to the one on the right. "His name was Haim. They named me after him. Haim, Harvey, get it?"

"That's nice," I said.

"No, that's not nice," said Harvey with quiet sarcasm. "The three of them were sent to Auschwitz."

"Auschwitz?" I asked, trying to make sense of what he was saying. "You mean like in *Holocaust*? I saw it on TV."

"Same old story," said Harvey, setting down the photo with an abrupt clink. "It's a bore, isn't it?"

"Harvey!"

"Oh, you're interested? Well, then I'll continue. But stop me if you want a commercial break. When the Americans freed Auschwitz, they found my grandmother, helped her get well, and helped her get to New York, where she married my grandfather, another refugee. They had a baby, my father, the man you just met."

Harvey sighed and went on as if he had to recite a tedious tale. "When my father was fourteen, he got into Stuyvesant. You know Stuyvesant?"

"No."

"I didn't think you would. Stuyvesant is a very good high school in the city. You have to be smart to get in. My grandmother walked him to school every day because she was afraid something would happen to him on the way. He began to wish he had a normal mother who made him peanut butter and jelly sandwiches and let him hang out with other kids. When he graduated, he went off to art school, got a part-time job, and found his own apartment."

Harvey stopped talking and walked out into the hall.

"What happened next?" I asked.

Harvey glared at me as if everything he was telling me was somehow all my fault. He sat down on the top step, and I sat down next to him. Harvey continued. "My father got married, my parents had me, they made money, we moved to Riverside Drive, and only very rarely did we ever go downtown to see my grandparents," he said. "They never came to see us either. I hardly knew them. Once a year we'd visit two shriveled-up old people in a dark, smelly apartment, and I'd have to kiss their wrinkled, whiskered faces."

"Oh, Harvey, the poor things."

"Poor things. That's easy for you to say. All they ever did was complain about the noise their neighbors made. My father gave them money, but they wouldn't use it. When my grandfather died, my father invited my grandmother to live with us, but she wouldn't leave her apartment." Harvey looked at me suspiciously. "Am I boring you?"

"Stop asking me that!" I said. "What happened to her?"

"As I said, two years ago she died. My father got depressed. He couldn't work. He went to a psychiatrist. That didn't help. Then one day, lo and behold, he got religion, and he could function again. It's a real miracle, see? As long as we celebrate every obscure Jewish holiday, he's fine."

I put my hands under my thighs and pressed my fingers down into the soft rug. At the bottom of the stairs was a bouquet of dark purple flowers I had never seen before. "Harvey," I said, "what happened to your grandmother's brothers?" I thought for a minute. "To your Great-uncle Haim?"

There was a long silence. I think we both were staring at those purple flowers. "Gassed," Harvey finally said. "As you said, just like in *Holocaust*."

"That's the worst thing I ever heard of," I whispered.

"I know it's awful," said Harvey, "but I don't want to build a stupid hut in the backyard just because something awful happened long ago. If my father wants to build it, fine. But do you think, Lisa, I should have to help? I mean, no one, but no one, builds sukkahs in backyards anymore. I doubt if my grandmother ever even built one."

"Well," I said, "in a way I can understand how your father feels. The more Jewish he is, the more connection he feels with his mother and uncles. It's not like he's doing the sukkah to bug you."

Harvey got up abruptly and went back to the window seat that looked out over the backyard. "Look," he said, lifting the seat.

I got up and went over. In the space under the seat were blankets, and under them, pushed to the side by Harvey's arm, was a rifle and a red box of rifle shells. Harvey slammed down the window seat and went into his parents' room. In the drawer of their night table he showed me a small black pistol.

"Actually," said Harvey, slamming that drawer shut too, "when you come right down to it, my father's not that crazy. I mean, there *is* a Nazi party in America. It's not so stupid to have a plan for self-defense. My father and I took shooting lessons in New York." Harvey seemed a little proud of this.

"But there aren't any Nazis in Bar Ferry," I said.

"How do you know? Last year they were trying to hold a parade in Connecticut. My father and I saw it on television."

"I don't know about that," I said.

Harvey looked at me as if I were a moron and ran downstairs.

• 15 •

I ran downstairs too, grabbed my things, and ran out to catch up with Harvey, who was on his way to the bus stop as if he were taking the bus, not I.

"Harvey," I said, "I'm glad you told me everything. It helps me understand you."

Harvey shrugged. I had to walk fast to keep up with him.

"I've made up my mind," he said angrily. "I'm going to tell my father, point-blank, that I'm absolutely *not* going to help him make the sukkah."

"Well, you have to do what you think is right," I said. "Parents can be impossible."

"Yeah," said Harvey. "Someone should exterminate them."

It was a horrid thing to say, but we both cracked up. Then Harvey got serious. "Lisa, the reason I told you all that was that I wanted you to know why I could never date you."

We were standing by the bus stop. "What do you mean?" I asked.

"I mean, if I went out with you, my father would stop eating and sleeping. He's impossible, Lisa. That's why I've been rotten to you. So you wouldn't like me."

I shook my head at the white stripe in the middle of the road. "That was really dumb," I said. "And anyway, if you knew you couldn't date me, why did you ask me to dance that night? You must have known I wasn't Jewish."

Harvey shrugged. "I just did," he said sheepishly. "No, probably the reason I did it was that my father made me go to temple before the dance and I wanted to get back at him."

The bus was coming. Harvey put his hand on top of my head and pulled me toward him. Just as the bus door opened, he kissed the side of my forehead. "And besides," he said, "there was something about you I liked."

· 16 ·

On the way home I stopped at the library. When there was no one around her, I went up to Miss Smith and asked in a half whisper, "Do you have books about Jewish people?"

"Jews?" she shouted.

"Yes," I whispered, wanting to disappear, "for a report."

"Israel or concentration camps?" shouted Miss Smith. "Speak up!"

"Um, I, ah."

"Which is it? Those are the usual topics!"

"Um, concentration camps," I said. "Auschwitz."

"Oh, Auschwitz. You're in luck. We have plenty on Auschwitz. Good thing you didn't get one of those minor camps." Miss Smith clicked her high heels across the main hall and into the big reading room. As we entered, I saw heads go up, but I didn't look at anything except the back of Miss Smith's burgundy pantsuit.

She stopped in the corner and waved at a row of books. "You ought to find everything you want to know about Auschwitz here," she said, loud enough for everyone in the room to hear.

"I read *Anne Frank*," I whispered.

"Of course you did," she said. "Too bad your report isn't on Israel. Then you could read *Exodus*. You'd like that too."

I pulled out a book with small print and no pictures. I had heard of *Exodus*. Some kids read it for book reports and said it was a great story. It seemed like a better idea than books on concentration camps.

"Is *Exodus* here?"

"That's fiction!" Miss Smith practically screamed. "And I told you that's Israel! You kids! Sometimes I don't know! See *U* on the other side of the room!"

"*U*?"

"*U* for Uris! Leon Uris! He's the author! Haven't you ever heard of Leon Uris?"

I stayed up all night reading *Exodus*. The next day I was a wreck. I didn't speak to Harvey because we ignored each other according to plan, but when we were finally down in his basement, laying out the dog's backbone, I said, "I couldn't sleep last night."

"What was the matter?" Harvey asked, as if he had forgotten all he told me.

"I read *Exodus*."

Harvey looked at me skeptically.

"It's awful the way the English treated the Jews after World War Two," I said.

"You mean the Nazis."

"No, I mean the English and the Balfour Declaration and the partition of Palestine so the Jews could have a homeland."

"Oh, that. How do you feel about the Palestinians today?"

"The book wasn't about today."

"You and my father would get along great." Harvey laughed and added nonchalantly, "I went to Israel."

"You went to Israel?"

"Yeah."

"Did you like it?"

"It was all right."

"Was it like it was in *Exodus*?"

"I never read *Exodus*."

"Harvey!"

Harvey shrugged.

"You really should read it."

"Why should I? All those Jews want to have their own country so they can all live together and kick everybody else out. It's a crock. Sorry, Dad." Harvey looked up at the ceiling.

"Harvey, how can you say that?"

"I just can, that's all. It's a crock. Did I get struck with lightning? Now let's get these vertebrae wired together."

I held out the thin wire Mr. Hanson had given us, and Harvey slipped on the first vertebra as if he were stringing a necklace.

Sometimes when Harvey talked tough, I knew he was putting it on. Other times, like now, I liked the way he could think for himself.

We wired the vertebrae together, leaving a little space between each one to indicate the tissue that is normally there. Working carefully, we added the tailbones at one end and the dog's small skull at the other. Harvey put the structure on a steel scaffolding Mr. Hanson had helped us make.

"It looks good," I said.

"I like the way the ribs stick out," he said.

"I like the way it makes me think about the bones inside me, how they work and move all day long yet I never think about them unless something goes wrong. Maybe people at the science fair will learn something from this poor dog."

"I like the things you think about," said Harvey. He put his hands on my shoulders and gave me a friendly little back rub; then he stopped and breathed into my hair.

"Lee," he said.

No one ever called me that except my father, so I turned around. The minute I moved, though, Harvey broke away from me.

"I have to watch out for you," he said, starting up the stairs.

Watch out for me? I wasn't doing anything! Harvey and I *never* did anything!

All he could talk about on the way to the bus stop were Mazdas and Honda Preludes. He wanted to know which car I liked best

because he'd be getting one soon. I said I
didn't know.

· 17 ·

With all that was happening between me
and Harvey, I was totally uninterested in
Donna's pajama party, but I knew if I didn't
go, Denise would never leave me alone. She
had been acting peculiar lately.

There were ten girls at the party, and at
midnight everyone wanted Clearlight to be
Sex Adviser, but she had different ideas.

"It's not that I don't want to do it," she
said. "It's just that I think someone else
should have a turn. After all, I'm not the
only one here who knows about sex, am I?"

There was an awkward pause, and then
everyone said no and changed her position on
the red-carpeted basement floor.

"I want to play Truth instead," said Clearlight. "But everyone has to promise to tell
the absolute truth." Clearlight was sitting
straight up and cross-legged like a dancer on
a black and white zebra-striped pillow. "Because, after all, the truth is all there is. I'll
go first. Who wants to say something true
about me?"

"You dress very well," said Beth.

"Don't just say good things," said Clearlight. The room was quiet except for the
munching of popcorn and the slurping of
sodas through straws.

Denise took a little, audible breath.

Clearlight looked at her.

"Well," said Denise, "I don't know if I should say this."

"The truth can never hurt anyone," said Clearlight. She said it in a way that made me nervous for Denise, who never seemed to understand the difference between being brave and being stupid.

"Well, sometimes you act, you know, a little superior."

Clearlight smiled. Denise cast a hopeful glance at me, but I couldn't support her this time.

Denise tried to amend her mistake. "I mean, I know that's only because you *are* superior. You wouldn't *act* superior if you *weren't* superior."

Clearlight cleared her throat and said, "If you believe I'm superior, I'm superior. If you believe I'm the same as you, I'm the same as you."

"Right!" said Denise. "That's what I mean, I think."

"Well, which is it?" asked Donna.

"Which is what?" asked Denise.

"Do you believe Clearlight is superior to you or the same as you?"

Poor Denise had sure worked herself into a hole this time. Clearlight was still smiling.

"I believe all men are created equal," Denise stammered.

"Men?" said Clearlight.

"People," said Denise. "Black, red, yellow, white, we're all the same inside."

"Why don't you go next?" said Clearlight, gracefully twirling and lifting off the zebra pillow.

Reluctantly Denise got up and sat down in place.

"You're a real sport," I said to cheer her up.

"And your hair is great," said Donna.

Denise beamed.

"But you could lose a little weight," said Ginger. "Say, ten or fifteen pounds."

"Don't say that! I can't help it!" Denise ran to the bathroom and came back with a red face. "I think Lisa should go next. I want to ask her something."

One thing you must never do in Truth is act afraid to go to the pillow, so I sat down and faced her, narrowing my eyes. "What do you want to know?" I asked.

Denise fluffed her pink flannel nightgown around her knees. She had completely recovered.

"Who do you like, Tommy or Harvey?"

"Tommy."

"Then why do you always stop talking to him at lunch and look around the cafeteria for Harvey?"

"I don't do that."

"You do too. And why haven't you called me all week to make plans for double-dating. I can't always be calling you."

I looked at her.

"And why don't you ask me what Bobby

said about Tommy's feelings for you? You just don't act like someone who likes Tommy."

"You mean why don't I go completely crazy over a boy like you do?"

Denise already sat on the pillow. "You can't ask her anything else now," said Beth.

Denise sniffed triumphantly.

"I've noticed you looking around for Harvey too," said Donna. "Do you expect us to believe that you go to his house every afternoon after school and just work on a science project?"

"He likes Ellen Goldberg," I said simply. "Don't you see them in the halls every day?"

"Maybe he likes two girls," said Clearlight. Everyone turned to her. She looked at me serenely and said, "The human heart is not always logical."

I knew I had to be careful. The worst thing in Truth is to blow it.

"I really don't care who Harvey likes," I said.

"He *is* a little weird," said Ginger, giggling. She glanced sideways at Denise, who started giggling too, as if they shared a secret joke.

"What are you two laughing at?" Donna asked.

"This is completely beside the point," said Denise, "but do you remember how Michael Rubenstein in fourth grade, you know, that little kid with the fat rear end, how he used to bring in funny crackers and pass them around the room during some Jewish holiday?" Denise and Ginger had become hysterical. "And wear a little black beanie? Well, Ginger and I were remembering that the other day, and I guess we just couldn't help thinking of it again."

Donna wrinkled her nose. "I remember that," she said. "God."

I could hardly believe I was right in the middle of an anti-Semitic conversation. This was what Harvey said went on in Bar Ferry, and I had denied it, like an ignorant fool. I couldn't believe Ginger and Denise. I bet they had been laughing at Harvey for weeks behind my back. I swore I would never, *ever* speak to Denise again. But I had to keep calm at the pajama party, so I shut my eyes, pulled that transparent lid over my brain, and wrinkled my nose just like Donna.

"You know," I said, "I don't know what you girls are getting so worked up about. You want to know the absolute truth? I'll tell you the absolute truth." I had a sense of déjà vu. Where had I had this conversation before? Oh, yes. On the stairs, with my mother.

"Okay," I said. "The night I met Harvey at the dance, I liked him. I let him walk me home and kiss me." I gave Denise a meaningful look. "But when I really thought about it later, I decided I liked Tommy because, well, how can I put it? He and I go together better."

"That's what I've been trying to tell you!" interrupted Denise.

"You were right," I said. "And Harvey and Ellen, they go together better than Harvey and me, do you know what I mean?"

She nodded happily.

"Harvey Burns and I, we're only close in a professional sense." I crossed my fingers in front of me and looked sincere. "I really hope we win the science fair. I've decided to become a surgeon, and first prize will help me get into a good premed school."

"Oh," said Denise, yawning. "Well, I hope you win too."

"Beth, you go next," said Donna.

"No, you," said Beth.

They were done with me, I realized with relief. One thing pajama parties are good for is realizing how well you can protect yourself against others when you have to.

· 18 ·

The next morning when I struggled back exhausted from Donna's, I found my father at the kitchen table with books and papers everywhere.

"What are you doing, Dad? Where's Mom?"

"She went to Alexander's. Said she had to go shopping to clear her mind."

I put my overnight bag on one of the kitchen chairs.

My father was shading in something with a green pencil. "This is grass," he said.

"What's grass?"

"See this, Lisa? Look. It's an earth-bermed house."

"A what? Wait a minute. Don't tell me yet. I have to make some tea to wake me up. Do you want some?"

"That'd be nice." My father looked up at me and smiled. As I waited for the water to boil, I leaned against the counter and listened patiently.

"I've been reading about these houses," he said, "but until now I hadn't worked one through for myself. This is the house of the future."

I looked at my father's sketch and saw a sliding glass door in the side of a hill.

"Where does that door go?"

"Inside the house," my father said.

"It's like a cave," I said.

"Somewhat," he said.

"A cave is the house of the future? Ugh-a, ugh-a." I tried to sound like a cavewoman. The kettle was whistling. I put a tea bag in a mug that had a map of Cape Cod on it and poured the hot water over it. "What did Mom need to clear out of her mind? Anything in particular?" I wondered if she had told my father about meeting Mrs. Burns and crying on the stairs.

"Mm-m? What?" My father was coloring again. "Oh, she just needed a little cheering up. See, Lisa, the way this house is built into the ground is so that you can heat it with just a few sticks of wood and a stove. The earth acts as the insulation and, because of the big door, you get solar heat too."

"Oh, Daddy," I said, transferring the wet half-used tea bag to a mug with a map of Maine on it. "People can't live in places like that."

"No? Look, it's already been done." He got up and held in front of me a magazine with a picture of a tired-looking family standing by a house that had grass on the roof. The headline was: "The Burgeoning of Berm." The subtitle said, "The Dunstables in Northern Washington State say they couldn't be more pleased with the home they built two years ago."

In the photograph the baby looked as if she were trying to get away from her father's arms. The mother was looking edgewise in a nasty way as if to say, "Can't you control her?"

"They don't look too happy to me," I said, carrying the mugs to the table.

"Well, it can work," my father said. "I just know it. We could all live in a house like this upstate somewhere. Get away from it all." He paused. "Be happy like we used to be."

"Oh, Dad," I said, "I think about that too."

"It's the time of year," my father said wistfully. "Your mom seems to get down this time of year. It was around this time her father died."

I hardly remembered when my grandfather died. I'd only been three. "But that was a long time ago."

"I know." He sighed.

"What's happening with her job?"

"Nothing good, unfortunately," he said. "I say quit it. Let's move upstate. We'll survive."

I wondered if my mother was tempted. I hoped not. "Dad," I said, "do you ever think about what the Nazis did to the Jews?"

"Of course I do. Everybody does. It was terrible."

"Six million of them were killed. Six million, Dad! How could the Germans have done that? How could they have made mothers, fathers, children, and old people take off their clothes and go into 'showers' to get gassed? How did the Germans do that, Dad? How did they get away with it?"

"I really don't know," said my father. "No one really understands. People try, but they just don't understand." My father furrowed his brows as he sipped his tea; then he went back to his coloring.

There was a stack of mail on the table, so I went through it absentmindedly. Macy's fall sale, Visa bill, nothing good at all, and then, suddenly, a smudged business envelope with my name and address written on it in red pencil.

"What's this?"

"What? Oh, that. I don't know. It's for you, isn't it?"

I slid my thumb under the unstuck part of the flap and tore the envelope open. Inside was a scrap of newspaper with something written in red in the margin. I looked at it unbelievingly and read, "Jew lover, you stink." Underneath was a red swastika.

· 19 ·

"Well, what is it?" asked my dad.

"Nothing," I said. "A joke. From one of the kids."

"You know what I wish I had? An electric pencil sharpener."

I told him to ask for one for Christmas, and then I ran upstairs. With a shaky hand I dialed Denise. Mrs. Hall answered.

"Well, hi, Lisa. She just got in, dead tired by the looks of her. Didn't you girls sleep a wink? Here, I'll put her on."

"Hi-ii."

"Denise, you tell me the truth. I mean, the real truth, not some game. Did you write that note?"

"What are you talking about?"

"Denise, this is important."

"I didn't write you any note."

"Did you get someone to? Ginger? Bobby?"

"No, I didn't get Ginger or Bobby to do anything. For heaven's sake, will you tell me what you're talking about."

"You know."

"I don't know."

"Swear on a Bible."

"How can I swear on a Bible about something I know nothing about?"

I hung up on her, went into my room, and reread the hideous note. Then I folded it up and thumbtacked it to the back of my bulletin board, where no one would find it.

I thought about calling Denise back and decided not to. I thought about telling my father and decided not to. I thought about calling Harvey and went back into my mother's room. I dialed his number.

"Hello?" It was his mother. "Hello? Hello?" I hung up. I would have to wait until Monday.

· 20 ·

But Monday Harvey was absent. I made a point of being friendly to Tommy and ignoring Denise. In home ec she passed me a note.

> Dear Lisa,
> I don't know what's the matter with you! What note? Are you mad because of the pajama party? I meant well. Honest.
> Your friend — I mean that *sincerely* — Denise.
> P.S. You're like a sister to me.

I didn't write back.

The next day the minute I saw Harvey I knew something was different. He had on a beautiful new brown ski sweater, but it was more than that. I had to look twice to see what it was. His braces were gone! Even though we rarely acknowledged each other in school, I couldn't help saying something.

"Harvey! You look wonderful!"

He was aloof the way he always was, but I could tell he was pleased. I could tell he was pleased on the bus too, even though he sat in the back. And when we got off at his stop, he grinned at me so! I hated to spoil his pleasure by showing him the note I clutched in my hand, yet I knew I had to get it over with.

"What have you got there?" Harvey asked.

"It's . . . I don't know . . . I'll show you inside," I stammered, looking at the patches of light and shadow that were skittering ominously across the street.

"What is it? A love note?" Harvey teased. "What are you looking so worried for? Do you think I've forgotten my promise to give you a real kiss?" Harvey smiled down at me, his teeth white and metal free. Suddenly he looked up, and his expression changed. "That's strange," he said. "Look. There's a light on in the basement. I didn't think anyone would be home today."

Harvey ran ahead of me into his house. When I got there, I found him coming down from upstairs. "I've searched everywhere. No one's here," he said. "My father must have come home earlier and left the light on." But Harvey still looked worried, and I was worried too, but not about the light in the basement.

"Whew, I'm sweating," said Harvey, trying to relax. He pulled off his sweater and tossed it on the hall table. Then he put out his arms to me. "Now do you want to collect on that no-braces kiss I promised?"

I couldn't put the note off any longer so I pushed the crumpled paper up between us. Harvey grabbed it with a looney grin. As he read it, though, his face turned red and angry. "It's Moose," he said, crumpling the note in his fist.

"No," I said. "It's Denise."

He looked up in surprise. "Who's Denise?"

"You know, my friend. At least she used to be my friend. The plump one with the red hair."

"Oh, her. What makes you think it was her?"

"Because she doesn't like you, and I've heard both her and her mother make anti-Semitic remarks."

Harvey looked surprised. "She does? Like what?"

"Oh, things like Jews are tribal and good at business."

Harvey frowned.

"Why do you think it's Moose?" I asked.

"He's a typical narrow-minded racist. A classic. But actually I don't think it's either Moose or your friend. The more I think about it, the more I think it's my father. He wants me to stop seeing you."

"But . . . we're not really 'seeing' each other. And anyway, I liked your father. He's a nice man. He wouldn't . . . it's absurd."

Harvey paced back and forth, ignoring my comments. "Lisa, listen. Don't say a word about this to anyone, you hear? You didn't already, did you?"

"I just asked Denise if she wrote it, but I didn't say what it was."

"Okay. Okay. That's okay. Just don't say any more. Did you ever hear of Spengler?"

"No."

"I think he was the one who said, 'If you don't have the guts to be a hammer, you'll be an anvil.' Did you ever hear of Masada?"

"No."

"It's a place in Israel where some ancient Jews wouldn't surrender. Lisa, we're not going to surrender. Do you hear? If you and I want to go out, no one can keep us from doing that, right?"

"Right," I said weakly. I was scared about the note but pleased to hear that it was true: We *were* going out. We *were* seeing each other.

"All right, look. I want you to go home. We're not going to work on the dog for a while. Then we'll see if the notes stop or continue."

"You mean I won't come here after school?"

"No, not for a while."

"But, if who ever wrote the note wants us to stop . . . going out, then they will have won. That makes us anvils, doesn't it?"

"We have to find out who it is."

"But how —"

"Just leave it to me."

"But if I don't talk to you in school and don't see you after school, how will you know if I receive more notes?"

Harvey stopped and stared at himself in the hall mirror. "If you get a note," he said grimly, "call me at eight o'clock that night. Let the phone ring once, then hang up."

I started to put on my jacket, but Harvey took it away from me. "Lisa," he said. His voice broke.

"What?"

"I just want you to do me one favor."

"What?"

He took my hand and led me upstairs to his room. My heart was banging against my chest. "Harvey," I asked, "what if your parents come home? What if they remember the light's on?" I don't know why I hadn't worried about his parents the other times I had been upstairs in his house.

"Don't worry," he said. "They won't."

We stood by his bed. "I just want you to do me one favor," he said again. "It may sound crazy, but it will help me get through this. It really will."

"What?" I barely got the word out.

He sat on the edge of the bed and tugged on my arm so that I sat next to him. "I have to know what it feels like to hold you. Just lie down next to me for one minute. That's all, I promise."

"Oh, Harvey," I said, but I didn't say no, and I didn't pull back. We stretched out, touching, in the center of his bed. I buried my head in his neck and thought: So, this is what it's like.

"Lisa," Harvey whispered, lifting my chin up and kissing my lips, kissing me more and more, opening up, warm and soft. Right then and there I knew for certain that I loved him and that for me Harvey was The One.

Suddenly Harvey rolled over and lay on his stomach on the far side of the bed. "I know I said one minute," he said, panting. "I know I promised."

"That's okay," I said. I put my hand flat on the back of his shirt and felt his body breathe up and down.

"No, a promise is a promise, Lisa." Harvey jumped up and shook the waistband of his pants. I jumped up too, and tucked in my blouse. I made my hair into a ponytail, then dropped it.

"Okay," he said with resolve, "we're going to have to be good actors in the days ahead. No one, I mean, *no one*, can know how we feel about each other. Go home and pretend you're not even thinking about me. We won't talk until the Halloween dance."

On the way home in the bus I looked out the window at all the familiar streets of Bar Ferry, the police station, the library, even the hospital where I was born, and thought: Not until I met Harvey did I realize that for fifteen years I'd been bored and lonely. I didn't feel that way anymore.

Part III

· 1 ·

The first thing I did when I got home was look through the mail and, sure enough, there was another one of those horrid, smudged envelopes scrawled with red lettering on the outside. I opened it up and read, "HITLER WAS A HERO. BEWARE."

I sat at the kitchen table, glad no one was home, yet at the same time terrified and wishing someone were. What did "BEWARE" mean? Would whoever wrote the note hurt me? But that was ridiculous because the suspects were Denise (she wouldn't), Moose (he might, but I didn't think so), and Harvey's father. I knew his father wouldn't hurt me. I went up to my room and thumbtacked the second note to the back of my bulletin board and wondered if I should tell my parents about it.

I went downstairs and scrubbed baking potatoes in a daze, half of me worried and upset about the notes and half of me dreaming about going out with Harvey. Maybe if his father knew we really loved each other, he wouldn't be so upset if we dated. I couldn't imagine that anybody would let something like religion upset him so, but of course, his was a special case. I was sure I would feel the same way under the circumstances.

When this whole mess blew over, I hoped I'd be able to sit down and talk with Mr. Burns. I'd ask to see some of the fans he designed. Maybe he'd like to see some of my best sketches. I'd tell him I had read *Anne Frank* and *Exodus* and how terrible they had made me feel. I would convert, I'd say. I couldn't believe he'd be as upset about me as Harvey imagined.

One thing I was sure of: The feelings between me and Harvey weren't going to go away. He was the most interesting boy I'd ever met. You couldn't stop two people from loving each other just on account of religion. Harvey was right about not being anvils. We would have to be hammers, that's all. In a way I looked forward to it.

When my father and mother came home, the potatoes were in the oven and I was opening a can of peas.

"Oh, Lord, I forgot and bought Chinese," said my father, setting a wet stained brown bag on the counter.

"Bill, we talked about it this morning," my mother said, exasperated. "I told Lisa we'd have hamburger patties."

"But I had an urge for Chinese food," said my father, "and thought we might have something a little special tonight. I got spareribs, dumplings, shrimp and snowpeas, and Szechuan beef."

I turned the oven off.

"How long have they been baking?" asked my mother.

"About an hour," I said.

"Well, take them out and throw them away. You can't do anything with leftover baked potatoes."

"We learned something in home ec," I said.

"There, you see?" said my father. "All is not lost. What was it, Lisa?"

"Coconut Potato Candy," I said. "You mash potato, coconut, and confectioners' sugar together, spread it in a pan, and cover it with melted bitter chocolate."

"Sounds delicious," he said.

"Sounds ghastly," said my mother.

I helped my father lay out the Chinese food boxes on the table. My mother brought over some plates.

"Bill, really," she said.

"It only cost eighteen dollars."

"Eighteen dollars is a lot of money."

"I love these dumplings," I said.

"I do too, when they're not so greasy," said my mother.

"Heather, sometimes you've just got to be a serendipidist," said my father jovially.

No one asked what that was.

My father got out a beer and asked my

mother if she wanted one. She said no. A few minutes later she got up, put one of the potatoes on a clean salad plate, and brought it to the table. She broke open the warm potato and started to eat it plain.

"More spareribs, Lisa?" my father asked.

"No, thanks, Dad. But I'll have some more shrimp. Want some more beef? The orange in it tastes good."

"Sure, pass it. Want some more rice?"

"Okay. Good idea."

My mother scraped the last bits of potato from the skin, got up, walked to the silver-ware drawer, and took out a small serrated knife. In my mind I saw her stop, turn, and say, "Bill, I want a divorce." But she didn't do that. She just came back and sat down.

"So how was your day today, Lee?" my father asked uncomfortably.

"Fine." How could I say that? It hadn't been fine. Part of it had been awful; part of it had been wonderful. It had been the best and the worst day of my life.

There was a long silence. My mother cut up the potato skin into small bits and ate them one at a time.

"Did you ever read *Exodus*?" I asked my father for the sake of conversation.

"A long time ago," he said.

"Did you like it?"

"It was okay."

"I loved it."

"It was a movie too."

"I'd like to see that. It's awful the way the Arabs are to the Israelis, especially after all Israel has done to make the desert bloom."

My father shook his head as he nibbled on the last sparerib.

"Israel is one of the most aggressive nations in the world," said my mother. "The Israelis treat the Palestinians the way we once treated the Indians."

"But if they didn't," I said, "the PLO would wipe them out."

My mother put a bit of potato skin on her tongue and nipped at it with her front teeth. "Since when are you so inerested in foreign affairs?"

"We study it at school."

"And at the Burnses' residence as well, I imagine."

"Sometimes we talk about it."

"You needn't be so snippy, Lisa."

"I wasn't . . . oh, I give up!" I said in despair.

"Well, I do too," said my father. "Honestly, Heather, you haven't said a pleasant word since you came in."

My mother set her knife and fork crosswise on her plate. "What do you expect? I have supper planned, and you come in with something different, and we're eighteen dollars shorter than we would have been if you hadn't got your 'inspiration.' If you wanted to indulge your inspirations like this, you should have stayed in advertising. But no, you quit that to collect cars and jars. I can't even put my pocketbook down on the counter because of all the jars."

My mother got up and went over to the counter. It was true. On the counter were rows of empty jars: mayonnaise jars, jelly jars, apple juice jars, peanut butter jars, pickle jars, and honey jars. "I've told you time after time, Bill, to put these jars in the basement!"

"All right, I will," said my father defensively. "I just haven't had the time to organize them yet."

"I'll show you how to organize them," said my mother. She was livid. "Just throw the stupid things away!" All of a sudden my mother started throwing jars into the garbage can.

"Heather, stop! I need them for more applesauce, and I'm going to try drying fruits and vegetables. It's crazy to have to go out and buy jars for that. Stop! I'll take them down to the basement now!"

But my mother wouldn't stop. She kept throwing jars into the garbage can. Some of them broke, but that didn't bother her. She kept going, half-crazed, as my father and I stared at her in shock.

When she filled up the can, she twisted the bag closed and, straining with all her might, hoisted it out of the can.

"Get the door, Lisa!" she commanded.

I jumped up, opened the back door, and watched in horror as my mother swung the heavy bag out on the back steps. It landed with an awful noise. In tears my mother came back into the kitchen and said, "Now at least I can find a place for my purse." She picked up her bag from a chair and slammed it onto the counter. Then she ran up to her room.

My father grabbed his car keys from his coat pocket and hurried out the front door. For a few minutes I stood in the middle of the kitchen and listened to him driving off and her sobbing upstairs. Then I turned on the back light and went outside to pick up the mess.

It took a long time and, although I touched lots of jagged glass, I didn't get cut. I tried to separate myself mentally from my parents. They weren't going to get a divorce; they were just going to fight like a bunch of kids. I felt older than they were. I certainly had graver problems on my mind. At eight o'clock I dialed Harvey, let the phone ring once, and hung up.

Every day for the rest of the week I got a note with a red scrawled anti-Semitic message on it. Every night at eight I called Harvey and gave him the signal.

At home we didn't eat any more meals together. My father ate as soon as he came home. I said I had to watch the news for current events so I might as well eat then. My mother hardly ate at all.

At first our new nonschedule was tense, but after a few days a strange kind of peace seemed to settle in our house. Like the lull before a storm, I suspected, wondering if my parents had discussed a formal arrangement. It was as if they were separated mentally but still living together. Whatever it was, my mother seemed happier.

One morning she actually reached over, patted my hand, and said she didn't see why families had to sit down together for supper, night after night. "It's better to face reality," she said. "There are times when each of us has to be alone. There's nothing wrong with that. Families ebb and flow."

I nodded as if I understood, but I didn't. I knew I didn't want my parents to get divorced, but I didn't want this ebb-and-flow business either. I wanted us to be happy all the time. My wishes, I realized, were pitiful, as unreal as a fairy tale, so I tried to set them aside and concentrate on my own problems with Harvey and the notes. The Halloween dance was approaching.

I was going with Denise, Bobby, and Tommy. We were walking. Denise had made all the arrangements, as usual, and I went along with them, keeping up the act. I was excited about the dance because I had the feeling that it would help Harvey and me find out who wrote the notes.

The way I figured it, it was either Moose or Mr. Burns. If Moose saw me dance with Tommy and Harvey dance with Ellen Goldberg all night, he'd probably give up and stop sending the notes. If the notes kept coming, it was probably Mr. Burns. I didn't suspect Denise anymore. She didn't stick with things that long.

I didn't know what Harvey thought because I hadn't talked to him in so long. But Harvey and I usually had pretty good telepathy, so I assumed he was trying to decide between Moose and his father too.

Before the dance Denise and I talked and decided to wear sweaters and knickers. I didn't worry about looking different anymore. I *was* different. That much I had come to see. I mean, who else was cutting up a dog and pretending she liked one boy when she really liked another?

When Tommy, Bobby, and Denise came to get me, I invited them in. I had told my parents the other kids were coming by, so my mom and dad were sitting in the living room, looking like a family in a TV commercial. My mother was knitting, and my father was reading the *Bar Ferry Evening News*.

"Mom, Dad, this is . . . well, you know everyone, don't you?"

"Hello, Denise, Bobby, Tommy," said my mother quite pleasantly.

"Hi, Mrs. Barnes," they said.

"No costumes?" my father asked.

"Nah," said Tommy. "They don't do that in senior high."

"So what's this about the swans?" asked my father.

159

"I heard something about that," said Bobby.

"What about the swans?" I asked.

My father began to read aloud. " 'Where are the Bar Ferry swans? All summer and fall they've made their home here. There were ten of them. Some people say five. Some say eight. They had a fine life here. But where are they now? Some say ten were found. Some say five. Some say eight — and shot and lined up in two rows on the bank south of the jetty. This is what people say. But who actually knows? Who saw them?

" 'Police are now investigating,' " my father went on. " 'Efforts are being made by many people to establish a reward fund that will lead to the arrest of the perpetrator. Mayor D'Daddio met with James B. Ford of the Environmental Conservation Office to discuss various allegations that the swans had been shot. Thus far no evidence has been found, but Mayor D'Daddio said the police will be pursuing several lines of inquiry. They ask that anyone who has evidence that the swans were in fact shot or who knows of anyone who actually saw their dead bodies get in touch with the local police.' "

"I heard a guy from the gas station say they were all lined up in a row," said Bobby.

"That's so gross I can't stand it," said Denise, putting her hands over her face.

"Weird," said Tommy.

"You never know what's going to happen next around here," said my mother.

"When I was a kid, we did some pretty bad things," said my father, "but we never did anything like that. Once we —"

"I'm sure the kids have to get going, Bill," said my mother.

"Of course." My father got up and walked us to the door.

We stepped out into the front light and walked down the winding sidewalk in pairs. I kept my hands in my parka pockets. Right now I couldn't stand to touch anyone.

· 2 ·

Beauty, Brighty, Beast, and Bay; Kathy, Darling, and Café. There were *seven* swans. There were always only seven swans. How could the reporter not know there were seven swans?

"I don't see how anyone could be so cruel," said Denise. "The swans were so beautiful. The thought of them dead makes me feel like crying."

"I imagine whoever did it had to be pretty good with guns," said Tommy.

"I heard something about that," said Bobby hesitantly.

"What did you hear?" asked Denise. "Bobby, tell us!"

"I don't know," he said nervously.

"Come on, O'Brien," said Tommy.

"Well, okay, it's just that I don't want to get Lisa upset."

I felt the sensation of cold mercury running over my skin.

Bobby looked back at me and then at Tommy. "I heard some guys after school, outside in the parking lot. They were saying that in gym kids were talking about what happened to the swans and how impossible it would be to shoot them all. And Harvey Burns kept saying you could do it if you had the right gun. He kept talking about different makes of guns, and then finally someone got sick of hearing him interrupt so many times, so he asked Burns how he knew so much about guns, and Burns said anyone from New York City knew a lot about guns."

"That's the most absurd thing I ever heard," I said firmly, trying not to sound agitated, trying to forget the clear image in my mind of the rifle in the window seat at Harvey's house.

"I'm just saying what I heard."

"If he did it, would he go around talking about it?" I asked. "He wouldn't say a word."

"He was probably just showing off," said Tommy.

"It's hard to move into a new town and make friends," I said.

"Yeah, especially when you act the way he does," said Denise.

"You don't even know him," I said.

"I do so. And anyway, why are you sticking up for him so much? I thought you didn't like him either."

"You know, Denise," I said more righteously than I could help, "you don't have to be in love with someone to understand him.

Throughout the project I've gotten to . . . know Harvey, and I'll tell you one thing I bet you've never even thought of."

"What's that?"

"Did you ever think how hard it might be for a Jewish kid to move into a town like Bar Ferry?"

"Lisa, that's ridiculous," said Tommy. "There are other Jewish people here."

"But not that many. You told me yourself Moose called him a kike."

"Moose," said Tommy in disgust. "You gonna let what Moose says bother you? He's a moron!"

"Look," I said. "Six million Jews were killed by Germans forty years ago. If you were Jewish, wouldn't that make you feel a little uptight?"

"Well, he probably *is* a little insecure," said Denise.

We stopped talking about it. Tommy reached over and took my hand out of my pocket. I smiled as best I could and tried to calm down.

· 3 ·

It was about eight thirty when we arrived at the dance. Surreptitiously I glanced about and saw that Harvey hadn't arrived yet. Then I remembered he said he had to go to temple Friday nights. I danced with Tommy and tried to have fun. Actually it wasn't too bad because, to tell the truth, standing around with Tommy and the other couples made me feel like an insider for the first time since school started.

At ten Harvey and Ellen Goldberg arrived. I swear they came in laughing. I wondered if they had driven from the temple to the dance together. Harvey had on a blue and white striped button-down shirt, and with his braces off, well, it just about killed me to see him having so much fun with Ellen. As they danced, they seemed to be having a wonderful time. What an act Harvey could put on! Surely Moose, who was in and out of the gym all evening could see that Harvey and I were not together.

Clearlight suggested we all get Cokes and go outside on the patio to drink them. Various other kids were out there too, cooling off in the dark fall night. Moose and his gang were coming back from the parking lot, looking pretty drunk. Maybe they got drunk every night and wrote those notes, I thought. That would explain the messy handwriting.

"If it weren't for training, I'd have a smoke," said Tommy.

"Why, Tommy DeNoto, I didn't know you smoked," said Clearlight. "Shame on you." She was the only one in the school who could say such a thing.

"I can't stand the taste of tobacco," said Rick.

"Cancer sticks," said Denise.

"True," said Tommy.

Out of the corner of my eye I saw Harvey

and Ellen come outside, laughing as usual. He had his arm around her shoulders.

Moose bellowed, "Hey, Harvey, had any target practice lately?" All the guys laughed.

For a split second I was terrified Harvey was going to start a fight; then his eyes shot over to mine as if he knew right where to find me. He put back his head and laughed at Moose and maybe at everyone. Then he and Ellen Goldberg turned around and went back inside.

Denise jabbed me with her elbow and hissed, "He looked right at you! There's something between you two. I know it!"

I lowered my eyelids as if to say, "Denise, how can you be so tiresome?"

But of course, she was right, and I began to feel more and more exhilarated as the dance went on. I knew Harvey would come up with some way for the two of us to be together. He had said he would speak to me at the dance. I could feel the adrenaline building inside of me. Sure as I knew my own name, I knew I wasn't going home with Tommy.

· 4 ·

"Okay, all you witches, goblins, warlocks, and wolverines, midnight is fast approaching, and the last dance is here. Happy Halloween, everybody, and remember this dance was brought to you by your friendly Student Alliance. If you haven't bought your membership yet, better do so now or you'll be turned into a toad."

As we danced, the side of Tommy's head was flat against the side of mine, the bones under my flesh next to the bones under his flesh. We rocked slowly, boringly, and I waited. Halfway through the record Harvey cut in.

"Hey!" said Tommy.

"It's important," said Harvey.

"You can't do this!" said Tommy.

"I have to tell her something," said Harvey.

"Let me talk to him," I told Tommy. "Something's been happening you don't know about."

"What? About the swans? I know all about that," said Tommy menacingly.

"No, not that," I said. "Really."

Tommy looked disgustedly at Harvey and then at me. I felt bad for him, worse than I thought I would feel, but still, I was glad Harvey had come for me at last. We went around the dance floor in our best style, but not close. I wondered if Ellen Goldberg was looking. And Clearlight. And Denise. And Tommy.

"I got one of those notes too," said Harvey, looking past my shoulder.

"No!" I forgot about everyone else and gave him a hug. "What did it say?"

Harvey looked grim. " 'Dog bones are Jew bones.' "

"That means it *is* Denise!" I said. "My first guess was right! Moose doesn't know about the bones!" I looked around the room for her and thought of punching her in the face.

Harvey sighed. "Lisa, I still think it's my father."

"Well, I don't. What you don't seem to understand is that Denise wants me to like Tommy so we can always double-date." I made a hissing sound to express my exasperation and anger.

"Come on," snapped Harvey. "Let's get out of here."

I figured I didn't have to say good-bye or apologize to anyone. It was people like Denise and her mother, who were like the Nazis, maybe not like the worst ones, but certainly like the ones who had turned their heads and looked the other way.

Denise's mother. The thought struck me. Was it possible *she* was writing the notes and not Denise? Hadn't Mrs. Hall brought up Harvey's name in a derogatory manner just the other day? Wasn't *she* the one who had gone on and on about the increase in the Jewish community in town? "I imagine they'll be hiring some fancy New York architect soon to build them a new temple," she had said. "I'm sure it will be very grand."

I stopped dancing and stared at Denise coming toward me across the gym floor, running and all beet red.

"Come on," said Harvey.

"Wait," I said calmly.

"Lisa!" cried Denise, with a flushed, accusatory look on her face. "Just where do you think you're going?"

"I'm going home with Harvey," I said.

"That's downright cruel," she protested. "What about Tommy?"

"Denise," I said, "there's something you don't know. If you did, I think you'd understand, but I'm not sure, and I can't tell you now. I'll call you."

"Come on, Lisa," said Harvey, pulling my arm. "Let's get out of here."

"Lisa!" shrieked Denise. "You're being terrible!"

"Denise, I'm sorry," I said firmly and steadily. I wasn't going to get hysterical like her. "Ask your mother about the notes when you get home. Tell her that I know and that I feel very, very sorry for all of you." With that, I turned and went out the door with Harvey.

"I'm sorry for you too, Tommy," I said to myself, starting on the way toward my house. Harvey was pulling me toward the parking lot.

"Where are you going?" I protested.

He didn't stop until the middle of the last row. There he stopped by the side door of a new white car. "*Entrez, s'il vous plaît.*" He smiled broadly. "I told you I was getting a car when my braces came off."

"This is *yours*?" Flabbergasted, I got in. The interior was maroon, spotless, and had the pungent, clean smell of new cars.

"Where to, mademoiselle?"

I shook my head in amazement. Harvey started the engine and drove out of the parking lot. I couldn't believe it. I thought of all the people who would be furious at me for doing what I was doing: Denise, Tommy, Ellen Goldberg, my mother, and my father. I had a sudden fantasy that they all were running after me, screaming at me, shaking their fists at me, but because I was in Harvey's new car, I couldn't hear them and couldn't see them unless I looked back, which, of course, I didn't.

· 5 ·

Cool as a cucumber, Harvey slipped a cassette into the tape deck and handed me the plastic box it came in. On the cover was a picture of a round-faced black woman. "You ever heard of Bessie Smith?" he asked.

I heard a woman singing, almost moaning, real slow and easy in a jazz way. I thought hard for a moment. "No, but I've heard of Dave Brubeck."

"Bessie's a blues singer," said Harvey.

We passed the Congregational Church in the middle of town, its steeple lit up pure white. "Nobody knows you when you're down and out," sang the woman, and I could tell she really meant it.

"Bessie knows about being an outcast," said Harvey, shifting gears smoothly to take a turn. "Dog bones, black bones. When she was dying, they wouldn't let her in the white hospital."

I don't think I can describe the sad feeling I had, riding in that brand-new car, listening to that black woman sing, and wondering why there was prejudice in the world. Every sensation I felt had a tragic edge to it: the sharp point of the steeple, the newness of the car, Harvey's hand gripping the gear-shift, the speed at which we were going.

I thought of my mother, probably on her Barcalounger, reading, and my father, probably working late in the basement. Their images didn't have much to do with what was happening. It was as if Harvey and I were on a runway taking off to a happier planet. I can't say I was surprised when Harvey pulled onto the parkway heading south.

"Have you ever been over the George Washington Bridge?" he asked, nonchalantly.

"When we went to California," I said matter-of-factly. Harvey turned off the tape and explained to me how suspension bridges are made. Later, he pointed out features of the bridge as we crossed it.

"You know so many things," I said admiringly.

"Stick with me, kid," he said, reaching over and resting his hand on my left thigh.

I can't explain how natural and wonderful that felt. I rested my hand on top of his. The only time I let go was when he had to shift, which wasn't often because we were flying down the New Jersey Turnpike.

"You know, Lisa," said Harvey, "people like you, me, and Bessie are different. It's like what she says. 'Nobody knows you when you're down and out.' I feel you're the only one who knows me."

"It's true," I said, caressing his hand. "I do know you." Most boys never thought about life's tragedies, but Harvey had to. "And you know me too."

I moved closer to Harvey, and he slipped his hand down a little more between my thighs. Everything felt natural. We rode in silence, and then I said, "Sometimes I feel a power in me. It's as if I am connected to every living thing on earth and all the stars and underwater creatures too. Do you ever feel like that?"

Harvey squeezed my leg. "Sometimes I feel like an eagle. I look down on the world and see everything from far away. People's problems look awfully small. I guess it's silly."

"It's not silly at all. You want to hear something silly? I have names for the swans. Beauty, Brighty, Beast, and Bay; Kathy, Darling, and Café. Ever since I met you, I wanted to tell you that."

Harvey didn't say anything.

I looked up at him. "Harvey, do you know

what some stupid kids are saying?"

"No, what are some stupid kids saying?"

"Some stupid kids are saying that you shot the swans."

Harvey stared straight ahead at the road. "What if I did? Would you hate me?"

I picked up his hand and held it in the air. "You didn't, did you, Harvey?" I whispered.

Harvey put both hands on the steering wheel. "What do you think?"

"I — I don't know. Those guns."

"Lisa," he said, shaking his head. "Don't you see? That was just another vicious, anti-Semitic incident. That rumor was started by whoever is writing the notes."

"That's right! Of course! Why didn't I think of that?" I felt like an imbecile.

"Maybe you have some doubts about me."

"No, I don't. I don't at all."

"Good. Then don't think about the swans. Think about Montana."

· 6 ·

"Montana?"

"I bet you thought I was going to say California."

"Not really. I wasn't thinking about states."

"Think about a little stone cabin in Montana with mountains in the background, grassy fields in the foreground, blue sky, and big white clouds."

"Do you own it?"

"No," he said, laughing, "but I sure can picture it."

I laughed too. "Well, in a way so can I."

Harvey put his hand back on my leg. "Of course you can," he said. "That's because you're a real woman."

That phrase "real woman" made me feel so alive, I can't tell you. For a long time we drove, fiery, quiet, and together. After a while it occurred to me that we were going pretty fast, so I glanced sideways at the speedometer. It read "85."

I thought about it and said in a friendly, easy way, "Well, this is one 'real woman' who doesn't need to go quite so fast."

"Don't worry about it," said Harvey.

"But, Harvey, why are you going so fast? Where are we going anyway?"

Harvey smiled at the road ahead.

There was another long silence, during which I began to get a little nervous. It was a crazy question, but finally I had to ask it. "Harvey, we're not going to Montana, are we?"

"We could."

The road was coming at us so fast I looked at the speedometer again. It said "90."

"Well," I said, trying to act as if nothing unusual were happening, "if we do, we'll have to eat first. I'm hungry, and look, here's an exit with a food/fuel sign."

"You read my mind," said Harvey,

swerving down the ramp much too fast. We turned down a side road and saw a diner and motel ahead, no names, just two brightly lit signs saying "Diner" and "Motel." Harvey pulled into a space in front of the motel.

"Harvey!"

"Only kidding," said Harvey. "But if we're going to Montana . . ."

"Harvey, we're not going to Montana!" I said.

"No? Oh. I thought we were." He shrugged, got out, and walked huffily toward the diner with me running after him. He selected the last booth near the windows. Except for a couple of truck drivers at the counter, the diner was empty. An old but nice-looking waitress with dark black hair and a short uniform came over.

"Hello. What can I do for you?"

"Nothing for me," said Harvey.

I looked at him strangely. "I thought you said —"

"You were the one who said you were hungry."

"You did too."

"How about a hamburger and a Coke?" asked the waitress.

"That sounds fine," I said.

"Me too," said Harvey.

The waitress wrote down our orders and left.

"Harvey."

"What?"

"Why are you like that?"

"What?"

"So . . . so, I don't know. So rude some-times."

"I'm not rude."

I folded up the scallops on the edge of the paper place mat.

"I don't know," said Harvey with a sigh. "I guess I'm upset about the notes. As Bessie says, I'm down and out. That's why I'm thinking of Montana."

"Not seriously."

Harvey looked at me as if he were really, really tired. "I wouldn't mind," he said simply.

"But we couldn't —"

"We could."

"Live in a cabin?"

"Why not?"

"But you said there is no cabin."

"We could build one."

The waitress came over and set down our food. "Will that be all, kids?"

"Don't call my wife a kid."

The waitress was shocked. So was I. Under the table Harvey kicked me.

"That's right," said Harvey. "We had to get married in ninth grade. The little one's at home."

The waitress stared at me. "Well, all I have to say is good luck. I'm sure you two make fine parents."

"Thank you," I said with a sad little smile,

going along with the act. "Would you like to see a photo?" Out of my wallet I took a photo of my baby cousin Marie.

"Will that be all?" asked the waitress after she had smiled pathetically at the photo.

"I think so," said Harvey. "We don't have much . . . money."

"You know what?" said the waitress, slipping her pad into her apron pocket. "Just forget it. I mean it, what the hell, pardon my French. You two relax and enjoy yourselves. This meal's on me."

"Nah, forget it," said Harvey, taking out his pigskin wallet. "We were just teasing." He took out a twenty and handed it to her.

The waitress shut her eyes and opened them. She took the twenty.

"Come on, Lisa," said Harvey at the cash register. "Let's go snort some cocaine." This time the waitress didn't even look up.

· 7 ·

When we got back in the car in front of the motel, I wondered what was next. Harvey looked at me mysteriously, then without a word slowly backed up the car and turned around in the parking lot. When he reached the road, he took off in a blast for the highway. Two exit signs were coming up fast on the right. Harvey slammed on the brakes and read them aloud.

"New York. East. One mile. Montana. West. One-quarter mile. Which will it be?"

"It doesn't say Montana," I said.

"No," he said. "But that is the way."

"Harvey."

"What?" He had stopped the car right in the middle of the road.

"You can't stay here. If someone comes, they'll hit us!"

Harvey lunged forward and hugged me so hard it hurt, "Lisa," he said. "Lisa, Lisa, Lisa."

"Harvey," I managed to say, "this is ridiculous! We're in the middle of the road!"

"You want to go back to the motel? You want to go to Montana? I'll do whatever you want." Harvey let go of me, pushed in the cassette, and leaned back in his seat. Bessie started singing again.

I pushed the eject button. "Harvey," I said, surprised at the shaky determination in my voice. "Get on the highway going east. I don't care what's waiting for us there. We have to go home."

Harvey took off so fast my head bounced off the head rest. As he took the curve on the eastbound ramp, I had to hold onto the armrest.

"Slow down!" I finally yelled. "We could get killed!" But it didn't do any good. We were already at sixty, and the speedometer was climbing. All right, I decided, the best strategy with Harvey was to ignore him. At least we were headed in the right direction. I pushed the tape in and shut my eyes. I heard Bessie sing a song called "I'm Wild About That Thing." Halfway through the song it occurred to me what Bessie was singing about, but I didn't let on I knew.

Mostly I was sad about the way I felt when Harvey grabbed me. He was like a stranger and a not very nice stranger at that. I glanced sideways at him and saw him jutting his chin out in a hard way I had never noticed before. We were going eighty.

"I'll thank you not to give me any more of those saintly sighs," said Harvey out of the blue. "That's one of the many things about you, Lisa, I don't particularly care for."

"What are you talking about? I didn't sigh."

"You did too. I'm talking about the way you keep changing all the time. One day you're romantic; the next day you're cold."

I was outraged. "I can't believe *you,* of all people, are saying that. *You're* the one who is always changing. One day you flirt with me, and the next day you flirt with Ellen Goldberg."

"That was an act. I thought you understood that."

"Well, sometimes it didn't seem like an act."

"So you were jealous?"

"It's not that I was jealous. It's that sometimes you acted so . . . I don't know, unpredictable."

"He loves me, he loves me not. Is that all you could think about? Whether or not I loved you? Don't you understand the problems I have?"

I heaved my chest in exasperation. "Harvey," I began again, trying to calm down, "it's like in the diner. First you say you're hungry. Then you're not. Then you're nice to the waitress. Then you're not. Every time I begin to trust you, you do something crazy! Like tonight! We were going for a nice ride in your new car, and you have to spoil it by saying we're going to Montana."

"And you have to believe me."

"Well, you acted like you meant it! And then the way you pulled up in front of the motel. What am I supposed to think?"

"You think I hop into bed with just any girl?"

"What's that supposed to mean? Harvey, sometimes you make me absolutely furious!" Suddenly the seven swans came into my mind, and for the first time I really wondered if Harvey hadn't taken one of his father's guns and . . . Beauty, Brighty, Beast, and Bay; Kathy, Darling, and Café. He had never actually denied shooting them. I said their names like a prayer because for the first time with Harvey I was afraid.

"I don't know what to expect from someone as gullible as you," he said.

"I'm not as gullible as you think," I said, leveling my voice.

"Dog bones, Jew bones. It was that crazy note that started everything." Harvey pulled the note out of his jacket pocket and tossed it over to me. It landed in my lap, but I made no move to open it. Harvey reached up and turned on the overhead light. Finally I opened the note and read the red-smudged scrawl.

"The irony," said Harvey, "is that if I showed that note to my father, he would say, 'See? That's why I keep guns.' There's no way I can win against him. Either he wrote the note, or he'd be glad I got it."

I felt bad for Harvey, but I couldn't think of anything to say or do. Usually I could with him, but this time I couldn't because I was too nervous. Harvey tried to get something on the radio, couldn't, snapped it off. I guess he didn't want to listen to Bessie Smith anymore. That was the only tape he had.

As we flew over the George Washington Bridge, I pulled my jacket tight around me and shut my eyes, praying we would get home soon and wishing I could be put to bed like a baby. Since I knew what was ahead of me, the image was absurd.

· 8 ·

"Awake, Sleeping Beauty."

I sat up in terror, saw my house, and leaned back against the headrest with relief. Harvey cut the engine and glanced at me. "See you 'round, Barnes," he said. "Don't burn any down." Just then the front door of my house burst open, and my parents came running down the sidewalk. I was so glad to see them I almost cried.

"Lisa!" my father yelled.

"Where have you been?" my mother screamed. "It's 2:30!"

They opened the car door on my side, and both of them yelled at me at once. Suddenly, I wasn't so glad to see them anymore.

"Lisa, do you have any idea how worried we were?"

"We've been calling everybody!"

"We even called the police!"

"Where were you two?"

"Why didn't you call?"

"And I suppose you're Harvey Burns?" my father asked.

"Yeah," said Harvey. "I suppose I am." He leaned across me to speak to my father. "Say, Mr. Barnes, would you do me a favor? Call my folks and say I'll be right home? Tell them I lost track of time, okay?"

"Harvey," I wanted to scream. "Why are you being so obnoxious? You should be as polite as you can be!" I got out of the car and slammed the door.

"What do you mean, 'lost track of time'?" asked my father, outraged.

"Never mind," said Harvey with a grin. He gunned the engine and took off in a roar, leaving the three of us staring at his white car until it rounded the corner with a screech and passed out of view.

"Did that boy do anything to you?" my father asked in a low voice.

I shook my head no.

"I never did like him," snapped my mother.

We walked up the curved S sidewalk to the front door three abreast with me trapped in the middle. The VW on the lawn looked like a beast curled up for the night. I wanted to curl up and sleep too, but that was impossible. I pulled the imaginary lid over my brain so I could get through the ordeal ahead.

By the time I reached the living room, I was in a trance. I listened to my father's voice explaining to the police that their help was no longer needed. I watched him sit down next to my mother on the couch. I heard him say, "All right, young lady, you'd better tell us everything."

I sat forward and stared at two worn spots on our rug. Once during a World Series game between the Yankees and the Dodgers my mother had become so excited she had kicked away the pile with her heels.

"Lisa!" said my father sharply.

His voice disturbed my detachment, and I began to waver between two states. Most of me said, "Wait, endure, float. Eventually they will be quiet and go away." But part of me was defecting. Part of me wanted to tell them everything. I tried to pull the lid more securely around my brain.

There was an awful silence, and then my

mother shot up from the couch as if she could restrain herself no longer. For a second I thought she was going to spring across the floor and attack me.

Instead she gripped her elbows with her hands and shouted, "Lisa, I've told you time and time again to come home when I say and by the method we'd agreed upon. What do you mean by defying me this way! Have you no consideration at all? How dare you not call? How do you think your father and I felt? We didn't know where you were! We didn't know what you were doing! We don't know that boy! Denise told us about the swans! He could have killed you too!"

Her last words startled me, and I looked up. In her eyes was more worry than anger, and I felt terrible. She was right. I could have been killed. Tears of fear, relief, and exhaustion began to flood over my eyelashes and stream down my face.

Suddenly my mother's hands left her elbows and gestured helplessly in the air. Then, somehow she was kneeling on the floor in front of me, and she was crying too. I grabbed her neck and fell on my knees sobbing. My mother wrapped her arms around me and rubbed my back. "Lisa," she said, "I'm —" But her voice caught in her throat and she had to wait a moment. "I'm sorry, Lisa. I'm sorry to yell at you that way, but you have to understand, my darling. You're the only child I have."

"I'm sorry too," I said, and I meant it.

"That's okay," she said. "You really feel wretched, don't you?"

"Yes," I said. I wanted my mother to hug me forever, but our knees were in the way so I sat back against the chair and wiped my eyes.

"Maybe I should make some hot cocoa," said my father gently. "How about that? Wouldn't that be a good idea? Let's go in the kitchen and talk."

My father took down the Connecticut, Vermont, and Maine mugs and set them in a row on the counter. Carefully, he measured cocoa mix into them while the milk he had poured into a saucepan was heating on the stove.

My mother's hands were spread flat upon the kitchen table. They were wrinkled and veined, yet surprisingly strong looking against the blue plastic tablecloth. On her finger was a small worn wedding band.

"Why don't you begin, Lisa?" my mother suggested.

I searched the room for a clue to help me start telling my parents about Harvey. I don't know what I expected to find, but what I saw was another one of those notes propped up against the back of the counter where the jars used to stand.

"When did that one arrive?" I gasped, rushing over to it. I tore open the by now familiar envelope addressed to me and read aloud: " 'Kikes kill swans.' Mom and Dad, this is the seventh letter I've received like this! I'm not kidding! Harvey got one too!"

"Let me see that," said my father. Both my parents stared at the note.

"I'll get the rest of them," I said, running up to my room. I hadn't thought to tell them about Harvey by starting with the notes, but I realized that they made the whole story and everything Harvey and I'd done comprehensible.

· 9 ·

Gravely we sipped chocolate and stared at the seven red notes spread out on the kitchen table. I told my parents why Harvey and I had gone on a long ride, how Harvey had been so upset that he wanted to run away to Montana, and how I had said we had to return home. My father said he was proud of me. I didn't mention the motel or the waitress who believed we were married.

My mother asked me if I thought Harvey had killed the swans, and I said that I didn't think so but that I didn't really know. I said it could be that whoever was passing that rumor around was the same person writing the notes. But I admitted I was afraid he might have killed them out of rage. I told my parents Mr. Burns owned guns to protect his family in case Nazis ever gained strength in America, and I told them all about Harvey's grandmother so they would understand the reasons for Harvey's father's fear.

My parents listened, astonished, to every word I said. Both of them were very upset.

"This is serious," my father said when I was finished. "Very serious. Who do you think wrote those notes?"

"Do you suppose there *is* an underground Nazi party in Bar Ferry?" asked my mother. "It's hard to believe but . . ."

"I don't really think so," I said.

"Who do you suspect?"

I looked at the foamy gray-brown remains of the cocoa in my cup and was embarrassed. "Denise's mother," I finally said.

My mother looked at the ceiling. "Mrs. Hall? What makes you think it was her?"

"She and Denise never wanted me to like Harvey, and sometimes she made derogatory remarks about Jewish people."

"Well, I can't say I am surprised," said my mother with a sigh.

"But you said Harvey thought it was someone else?"

"He thought it was his father," I said. "Or maybe a kid named Moose."

"His *father*?"

"I know it sounds crazy, but Harvey thought his father might be doing it to make me dislike Harvey."

"Why would he want to do that?"

I shifted my position on the chair. "He doesn't want Harvey to date non-Jewish girls."

"So you two *were* dating," said my mother, but not harshly. "I thought you told me you didn't like Harvey."

I shook my head sadly at the tablecloth. "First I thought I did; then I thought I didn't; then I thought I did again. Do you know what I mean?"

"Yes," she said. "I do know what you mean."

My father stacked the notes one on top of another and folded them in half. "Monday morning we're going to talk with someone in your school about this. Someone who knows you kids well. I don't think we should call Harvey's parents until after that."

"Who would you recommend at school, Lisa?" asked my mother.

I looked at the red maples on the *Vermont Life* calendar hanging on the wall by the window and remembered that Mrs. Burns thought I knew why trees change color in the fall. Suddenly it seemed presumptuous on her part to assume that just because I was smart, I knew everything.

"Mr. Hanson, I guess. The biology teacher. He gets to school early."

"Are Denise and this kid Moose his students too?"

"I don't know about Moose, but he has Denise in non-Regents biology."

"Then we'll go see him," said my father. "All of us. Together. First thing Monday morning."

I lay in bed and wondered how much trouble Harvey was in. I was so confused about my feelings for him I couldn't sleep.

Unable to keep my eyes open before, now I couldn't keep them closed.

There was a tap on my door.

"Yes?"

"It's me."

"Come in."

My mother came in and stood by my bed. "Are you too old for me to tuck you in?" she asked.

"No," I whispered.

"Good," she said. She went around both sides, neatly tucking my covers in. Then she said good night.

"Good night, Mom," I said. I was grateful that my mother knew what I needed. After she left, I fell asleep right away.

· 10 ·

Monday morning, when we walked in, Mr. Hanson was correcting papers at his desk. Next to him was a Styrofoam cup of black coffee and a half-eaten Danish on a piece of wax paper.

"Lisa!" he said with surprise. "What brings you here?"

"Mr. Hanson, these are my parents."

"Mr. and Mrs. Barnes. Is there something I can do for you?" Mr. Hanson rose and shook hands. "I've heard about your plans for a solar house, Mr. Barnes. Was thinking of you for a consultation. What's the matter? Is something wrong? Is it about the dog?"

"Not exactly," said my father. "May we

sit down?" My father was wearing the butterfly tie I had painted for him in fifth grade — two monarchs landing on a cattail.

We sat in classroom seats. I was feeling terrible because I was going to get Denise's mother in trouble. I hoped Mr. Hanson could think of a good way to deal with the problem. The only way the situation could get really bad, I figured, was if we found out that Mrs. Hall was part of a fledgling Nazi ring. But that sounded like TV, not real life, so I wasn't too worried. Maybe Mr. Hanson would just have a nice talk with Denise and her mother, after which Mrs. Hall could apologize to everyone. Then things would calm down.

"The thing is," my father began, "Lisa has been receiving notes in the mail." My father took them out of his pocket and handed them over to Mr. Hanson. "We think they might be written by a child's parent, but we're not sure. So we thought we'd talk to someone at school first. Lisa suggested you."

Mr. Hanson unfolded the notes and read them. He shook his head back and forth in consternation and asked me to tell him as much as I could about receiving them.

I told him my story, ending with a list of all the suspects. "I honestly don't think it's Harvey's father. I met him, and I like him. Denise doesn't hold grudges for long. As for Moose, I don't know, he just doesn't seem that mean. Mrs. Hall isn't mean either, but she knew about the bones and she's the most narrow-minded. Maybe you could just talk to her and get her to admit the truth and apologize."

Mr. Hanson got up, put his hands on his waist, and went to his desk. He looked at some papers; then he went to the door and stepped out into the hall for a few minutes without telling us why.

"He's very upset," said my mother.

"With good reason," said my father.

When Mr. Hanson came back, he said, "I've asked someone to join us. I hope you don't mind waiting until he can come." Mr. Hanson stood by his desk and finished his Danish in two big bites. He drank his coffee, crumpled the wax paper, put it in his cup, and threw them both in the wastebasket.

"How's the dog coming?" he asked.

"Good," I answered nervously.

In a few minutes Harvey walked into the room. "What's up?" he asked. "Someone said you wanted to see me."

"Sit down," said Mr. Hanson.

Harvey slid into a seat behind my mother. "Morning, everyone," he said.

My mother and father just looked at him. "Hi," I said. Mr. Hanson came over with a manila folder that said "Harvey Burns" on the tab. Without a word he passed each of us a sheet of paper from inside.

"What's going on?" asked Harvey.

"Just look," said Mr. Hanson.

It was a good thing I was doing all the note taking for our project, I thought, and not Harvey because his lab notes were pretty sloppy. Then I gasped.

"Harvey," I whispered.

Mr. Hanson set the red notes on Harvey's desk. "Even though you disguised your handwriting, it's not hard to match the red notes with the lab notes. Why did you write them, Harvey?"

"Those silly notes?" said Harvey with a laugh. He stood up. "It was a joke." He laughed again. No one joined him. "I don't know why everyone has to take everything so seriously."

I couldn't look up at him. I heard the bravado in his voice and knew he must be standing in one of his tough guy poses, staring at us as if we were fools. Shocked as I was, I also knew instantly why Harvey had done it. He did it because he was scared of how much he and I liked each other. He was the one trying to break us up. I understood, felt humiliated for him, and couldn't look up.

I don't think I'd ever felt more for Harvey than I did at that moment, but then I heard him say, "Lisa, I don't believe how gullible you are." He grabbed his book bag in disgust and started to leave.

"Young man!" said my father, rising.

"Let him go," said Mr. Hanson. "There will be time to deal with this. I'll have to talk with the principal, who, I imagine, will want to get in touch with his parents. May I keep the notes?"

"Of course," said my mother. "That was very clever of you to figure out that Harvey wrote them. I don't understand why he did, but, Lisa" — she turned to me — "you must be so upset."

I was, and worse, the implications were beginning to hit me like slaps in the face. He may have written the notes because he liked me, but he was willing to let others, like his own father and my friend Denise, be suspected. If he was crazy enough to write the notes, he probably *had* killed the swans. If he had killed seven beautiful, innocent swans, he could have done other terrible things. And to think I rode all through New Jersey with him.

"Lisa can be excused for the day," my mother said, putting her arm around me. "Can't she, Mr. Hanson?"

· 11 ·

On the way out to the parking lot my father said, "Whenever my uncle William had a problem, he went out for breakfast, even if it was four in the afternoon or nine at night."

There was a little silence, and then my mother suggested the International House of Pancakes.

"Do you remember how you always used to want to go here to eat?" asked my father.

"Yes, I do," I said.

"And how you insisted on putting all the different kinds of syrup on your flapjacks?"

"Yes, I do," I said.

After we sat down in a booth, my mom got up to call her office to explain why she was late.

"I'll just tell them the truth," she said. "My daughter was in trouble and I had to help her."

After she left, my father and I drank the orange juice that the waitress had brought for us.

"Well, I'm sure the police will be called in to investigate the notes and the swans too. That was some weird kid. How'd you ever get involved with a boy like that?"

"Will anything bad happen to him?"

"If he killed the swans, yes. As far as the notes go, I think he'll probably have to go to see a psychiatrist."

When my mother came back to the table, my father excused himself to call a VW dealer. My mother watched him leave, then turned to me. "Lisa," she said, "I'm going to have to leave in a few minutes."

"Aren't you even going to stay and have some pancakes?"

"I can't. Look, my boss is a royal pain, okay? He wants people at their desks looking busy all the time. He gets nervous when we take coffee breaks or come back five minutes late from lunch. He said I have to get right back."

My mother never talked to me like that. I think it embarrassed her. I smiled to show I understood and sympathized.

"Before I leave, I just want to tell you, Lisa . . . your dad and I, we love you."

"Mom," I said, amazed at myself for asking, "Mom, I've been wondering so long. I mean, here's what I really want to know. Please, just tell me. Do you and Dad love each other?"

My mother blushed and looked toward the hall where the phones were. My father was finishing up and heading back to our booth. "Oh, Lisa. Your father? Do I love him? Why, yes, I guess, I mean, of course, I *love* him. Why? Why do you ask?"

"Tell me the truth," I said quickly. My father had stopped at the counter to buy a paper.

For a moment I thought she was going to get mad, but she didn't. "It's so complicated," she finally said, her voice neither shrill nor whiny. "When you're older, you'll understand." She started rubbing her arms. "No, that's not fair, is it, Lisa? I'm going to have to tell you more." She looked at me, sizing me up. "You really got hurt by that boy, didn't you?"

I nodded and bit my lower lip.

My father came up to the table, looking pleased, and said, "I can see you two were having a nice chat."

"We were," said my mother. "But right

now, unfortunately, I have to go to work. You two have a nice day."

"I think I'll go back to school," I said. "I may as well face it."

She smiled at me. "Good luck," she said.

"You too," I replied.

· 12 ·

"Denise," I said as we were entering home ec, but she didn't answer. As I expected, she wasn't talking to me. Neither were Tommy and Bobby.

So, while Mrs. Jennings discussed the three principles of making mayonnaise, I wrote two notes:

> Dear Denise,
> I know you are mad at me because I left with Harvey after the dance and also because I said something about some notes. I want to apologize. It had nothing to do with you or your mother. I hope you will still let me be your friend.
>
> > Sincerely,
> > Lisa

and

> Dear Tommy,
> It's hard for me to explain what happened Friday night, but I know it wasn't right, and I'm sorry I did it.
>
> > Honest,
> > Lisa,

Denise wrote back right away and said, "Quite frankly I'll have to think about it."

I could tell that Tommy was spending all period debating what to say. Finally he wrote, "It's okay. I took Donna home. Personally I don't know what you see in a guy who would do that to swans."

After biology Mr. Hanson told me Harvey had gone home and wouldn't be back in school until after Thanksgiving vacation. He said that his parents had brought everything concerning the dog project to school when they came to pick Harvey up and that it was all in boxes in the supply room. I could finish the project myself if I wanted. Harvey could no longer be involved. That was part of his punishment, his parents had said.

"I don't know if I want to do it," I said.

"Think about it. I think I would if I were you," said Mr. Hanson. "I took a look at what you've done, and it looks swell. It's too bad what happened, but you know, it's probably best for Harvey. He's got some problems, but I imagine he'll do just fine someday."

I looked at Mr. Hanson doubtfully.

"Sometimes," he continued, "kids go through difficult times, that's all. Especially kids your age. With a little help you can use those hard times to learn about life."

"But what about the swans?" I asked.

"What about what swans?" Mr. Hanson asked. He lived three towns away.

"There was an article in our town paper saying someone might have shot the ones that come to the Bar Ferry dock. Kids are saying it was Harvey. And the last note Harvey wrote said, 'Kikes kill swans, beware.'"

Mr. Hanson laughed. "That's ridiculous," he said.

"They're gone," I said.

"Sure. It's getting cold out. They've migrated, that's all. You mean people *really* believe they were shot?"

"A guy at a gas station said he saw swan bodies lined up in a row on the beach."

"How many?"

"The paper said eight to twelve, but I know there were only seven swans at our dock."

"Do you really think someone could kill more than one swan from a flock? It's impossible. The others would all take off. And you'd have to be a pretty good shot to kill even one. Anyway, no one would do it. They're not birds that are hunted. It's the most ridiculous thing I ever heard."

So Harvey wasn't insane. The only thing he did was write the notes, and all that would happen to him was that he would go to a psychiatrist. I was immensely relieved. "Mr. Hanson," I said, "would you do me a favor?"

"What's that?"

"Could you say what you just told me in your classes? I think that would stop the rumor."

Mr. Hanson said he would be happy to, and I left his room thinking: Beauty,

Brighty, Beast, and Bay; Kathy, Darling, and Café. I'll see you in the spring . . . if you come back to Bar Ferry.

Two days later Ellen Goldberg stopped me in gym and asked if I'd heard that Harvey and his parents had gone to London for Thanksgiving. No, I said, I hadn't heard that. She said her mother had taken the Burnses to Kennedy Airport. I said great. She seemed pleased to have delivered the news.

· 13 ·

For Thanksgiving we took my grandmother out of the rest home and brought her to the Homestead, a big restaurant with picture windows that looked out over the Hudson River. It was very crowded, and Grandma didn't like the waiter. "He should keep refilling the water glasses," she said. "Things aren't like they used to be."

My mother and father tried to interest her in other subjects, but mostly she just liked to watch and criticize the waiters. We got home early.

I guess I was surprised when Denise called and said her mother invited me over for their dinner, which was going to be in the evening. I said I'd come by.

When I arrived, they had finished the turkey and were eating a striped Jell-O salad. "Red, white, and blueberry," said Mrs. Hall, "for the Pilgrims. Would you like some? If you want, you can have turkey too, but we've already finished the main course."

"Betsy Barton Hall, you are the best cook in the whole wide world," said Mr. Hall. He got up, walked around the table, wiping his mouth with a pink flowered cloth napkin, and gave Mrs. Hall a big kiss on the cheek.

"I love trying new things," said Mrs. Hall, pleased as could be. "So what happened to that boy, Lisa?" she suddenly asked me, just like that. I thought: I'm glad my mother isn't so nosy.

"Who? Harvey Burns?"

"Yes, Harvey Burns." She looked at Mr. Hall and said, "We're talking about the boy Lisa was cutting up a dog with. For a while we thought he murdered ten swans."

"Sounds like a real winner, Lisa," said Mr. Hall.

"I'm doing the dog skeleton for the science fair myself," I said, "and he's in London with his family."

"My, my," said Mrs. Hall. "London."

I was secretly proud of Harvey for being there. I wondered if Harvey ever thought of me anymore. I wondered if he was worried about having to go to a psychiatrist.

"He's a very interesting boy, I gather, from everything Denise has told me," said Mrs. Hall.

I looked at her and nodded. "That's right, Mrs. Hall. You said it exactly. He *is* very interesting."

I knew Harvey would be pleased at the way I turned her condescending remark around and fired it right back at her.

"You don't seem sad," Denise said to me upstairs when we were alone.

I was genuinely surprised. It was one of the most perceptive comments Denise had ever made. Maybe she wasn't so dumb after all. She was sitting cross-legged on her bed, hugging her Snoopy pillow. Maybe someday she would even toss out her Snoopy things.

"Sad?" I said. I was sitting at her dresser, looking at myself in the mirror. I didn't look so bad considering all that had happened to me. Maybe I would get a new haircut. "No, I'm not sad it's over. He was a boy worth knowing, if you know what I mean."

Denise sighed. I think she had finally realized that Tommy and Bobby were on one level and Harvey was on another.

"But Tommy has his good points too," she said.

"I know." I sighed. "That's why I still like him."

"You still like him? But what about Donna? Do you think he likes her?"

"I don't know. What do you think?"

We spent the rest of the evening analyzing the relationship between Tommy and Donna.

· 14 ·

After Thanksgiving vacation Harvey came back to school, breezy and self-confident as if nothing had happened. I suspect he knew all along that the swans had migrated. For a month he didn't drive to school because, I think, he was being punished. Then he drove every day. His car always looked clean.

Harvey never came by Mr. Hanson's class after school to see how I was doing on the dog, which, by the way, won first prize locally, third prize at the county fair, and no prize on the state level. I still have the skeleton packed in Styrofoam peanuts in a box in the attic. Also in the box are the photo of Harvey and me dancing, my sketch of Harvey, his "Someday" poem, and the little wooden fish pin.

Harvey and I never spoke again. For the rest of the year he went out with Ellen Goldberg and I went out with Tommy. If we passed as couples in the hall, it was as if the other couple were invisible.

I never told anyone else about the notes. Basically everything was over the day I found out who wrote them. Yet something still lingers between me and Harvey. No matter where I am in a crowd of kids, it seems that Harvey Burns is never far away. I can sense when he's around. In my peripheral vision I spot his head by its angle and motion, and when I turn to see if I'm right, his eyes brush mine, always, just for a second.

For Harvey Burns every gesture has a meaning. So when he looks at me that way, I know he misses me, and I'm sure he knows, because I turned to look, that I miss him too. It's true.

You don't just meet people out of the blue. Things happen for a purpose. The moment you're born, you start heading for the most important people in your life. Harvey Burns was an important person in my life, but that didn't mean we had to go together forever. Just for a while, when we were down and out.

About the Author

Jean Marzollo is the critically acclaimed author of many books, including Halfway Down Paddy Lane *(also available as a Point Paperback), a 1981 American Library Association Best Book for Young Adults. She has also written picture books, easy-to-read books, and books on child care. She lives in Cold Springs, New York, with her husband and two sons.*